PALEOJOE'S
DINOSAUR DETECTIVE CLUB

BOOK #3

SECRET
SABERTOOTH

Mackinac Island Press
for the love of reading

Other PaleoJoe Books

Dinosaur Detective Club Chapter Books

#1 The Disappearance of Dinosaur Sue
#2 Stolen Stegosaurus
#4 Raptors Revenge
#5 Mysterious Mammoths

Hidden Dinosaurs

...and more to come...

Published by Mackinac Island Press, Inc.
an imprint of Charlesbridge
85 Main Street
Watertown, MA 02472
(617) 926-0329
www.charlesbridge.com

Library of Congress Cataloging-in-Publication Data on file
PaleoJoe's Dinosaur Detective Club #3: Secret Sabertooth

Summary: PaleoJoe and the Dinosaur Detective Club follow clues to help their new friend Sarra find her missing brother and solve the mystery of a unique Sabertooth skull which leads them to La Brea tar pits.

ISBN 978-1-934133-10-1

Fiction

Printed and bound January 2010 by Lake Book Manufacturing, Inc. in Melrose Park, Illinois, USA
10 9 8 7 6 5 4 3

Dedicated to the imagination
and discovery that
all children have with dinosaurs.

SECRET SABERTOOTH

TABLE OF CONTENTS

TABLE OF CONTENTS

CHAPTER ONE

DAKOTA'S NIGHTMARE

Heavy air suddenly pushed into the interior of the small plane as PaleoJoe pulled open the door. The wild wind whipped the brim of his hat into a crazy, floppy dance as he gave Dakota the thumbs up.

This is it, thought Dakota. It was all happening very fast.

Dakota cinched the shoulder straps of the pack he wore tighter about his shoulders. The pack contained his parachute and it would be his only lifeline when he jumped out of the plane.

It's now or never, he thought.

With a brave, but slightly lopsided grin at PaleoJoe, Dakota launched himself out of the plane. He belly flopped on empty sky and the hard wind tore at his clothes. Above him, with a buzzing roar, the plane zoomed away leaving him alone, falling through the roaring air.

Dakota reached to pull the ripcord that would deploy his parachute. It wasn't there! Fear gripped him with suffocating force. His hand frantically scrabbled at the front of his jacket but there was no cord to be found.

And then, panic crawling in the pit of his stomach, he realized the truth. Somehow before he had jumped out of the plane, Dakota had mistakenly put on his *backpack* instead of his parachute! Fear rocketed through his body and seemed to explode from his head. He felt like he was choking on the heavy air that pushed into his face as he fell. And the ground below was getting closer.

What could he do?

Just then Dakota's school principal, Mr. DeLozo, fell in the air next to him.

"Mr. DeLozo, help!" Dakota tried to yell but the harsh wind tore his words away and all that came out of his mouth was a dry, croaking sound that no one could hear.

Mr. DeLozo, wearing a red and blue Hawaiian shirt with parrots and hula girls on it, and a pair of checkered shorts, kicked his white chubby legs in the air looking like a giant bullfrog and then did a somersault.

He's showing off, choked Dakota in disbelief. *I'm going to die and my principal is showing off!*

Mr. DeLozo grinned and suddenly, like a magician conjuring from thin air, produced a dart with a blood red feather. Dakota recognized it as one of the darts Mr. DeLozo had for the Discipline Board behind his office door. Mr. DeLozo took quick aim and threw the dart at Dakota.

Dakota cringed away as the dart flew past him, narrowly missing his face. Mr. DeLozo pulled his ripcord. Dakota could only watch as the parachute snapped open above his principal like a big mushroom, stopping Mr. DeLozo's fall, and whirling him away.

Great, thought Dakota. *As always, Mr. DeLozo was not so helpful.*

"Hey, Dakota!" Now it was Detective Franks who was swimming in the air beside him. "Smile!"

The flash of Detective Frank's large police camera burst in Dakota's face. Frantically, Dakota gestured to his friend trying to make him understand the terrible danger he was in. But Detective Franks only smiled and waved back as he pulled his own parachute cord.

"Detective Franks!" Dakota tried to yell, but it was as though his throat were stuffed with cotton. And, anyway, it was too late. Detective Franks became a small, fat dot far above Dakota, and Dakota continued to fall.

But then, suddenly, there was Shelly Brooks falling right beside him. Her red ponytail streamed straight up from under her pink, crash helmet. She

wore a pink jacket and pink goggles.

Thank goodness, thought Dakota. If anyone could figure out how to save him, it was Shelly. Next to PaleoJoe, she was the smartest person he knew.

"Dakota," she yelled at him now. "You forgot

your parachute!"

"I know!" he tried to scream back. "Help!"

"Sorry," yelled Shelly. "The ground is too close. Don't be so stupid next time!"

And Dakota watched in complete despair as Shelly pulled her ripcord and, with a snapping, sheet flapping sort of sound, her parachute bloomed above her like a giant, pink flower.

Dakota looked down. The ground was very close now. He wondered if when he actually hit the ground, he would go *splat-flat* like a squashed frog on the highway. But then, suddenly, in the distance he saw something that gave him a jolt of hope. Tiny, rectangular boxes far away on the ground began to get bigger and bigger. And soon Dakota was certain they looked familiar. It looked like the mobile home court he lived in.

It was!

And, look! He actually pointed, although there wasn't anyone around to actually see. Wasn't that mobile home with the green, corrugated roof his own home? Yes! It was! And what was that large, fluffy, white pile in his yard?

As he fell closer he could tell that it was a huge pile of sheets and laundry left out by his mom. This exciting discovery gave him new hope. Maybe, if he fell in that pile, he wouldn't die.

Dakota began moving his arms and legs as though he were swimming in the air. Somewhere above him he thought he could hear Shelly laughing at him, but he ignored it and kept on flailing his arms and legs.

It was working! The pile of laundry was definitely closer. He was going to make it! Dakota curled into a ball and went in for a landing!

CHAPTER TWO

OTHER WAYS TO FLY

Crash!

Dakota fell out of his bed in a tangle of sheets and blankets and hit the floor with a thud that rattled his teeth and shook him wide awake. His eyes flew open and with his heart still pounding, as though it would leap from his chest and go dancing across the bedroom floor, Dakota realized he had been dreaming.

"For crying out loud," he muttered to himself feeling the sweat soaking into his pajamas and gazing up at the bottom of his bed. This was the third nightmare he had had this week. And he knew why he was having them, too. His mother called them anxiety dreams and Dakota had an anxiety all right. It was a big one.

He snaked out his arm and felt under his pillow for a small, blue memo book that he kept there. When he found it, he flipped it open to the first page where he had neatly printed at the top: THINGS TO DO. Taking the small pencil from the white coil of wire spiral that held the notebook together, Dakota carefully wrote:

1. Learn to skydive
2. Tell Shelly about the essay contest

It was that second item that was giving him Anxiety with a capital A. Last month he and Shelly had both entered the Junior Paleontology Essay Contest sponsored by Cross Continental Airlines. The winner of thc contest would win two free airline tickets to any destination in the continental United States. Shelly had been sure she would win it. Dakota had been sure Shelly would win it. But she hadn't. He had. And he hadn't told her about it yet, and so it was giving him nightmares. One thing was certain, if Dakota didn't want to continue getting bruises on his backside from falling out of bed, he knew that he would have to tell her soon.

"Dakota?" His bedroom door opened and his concerned mother stood framed in the doorway. From where he lay on the floor, he could see her shoes and the cuffs of her dark pants. She was dressed for work.

"It's okay, Mom," said Dakota his voice muffled as he struggled to untangle himself from his bedding. "I just fell out of bed."

"Are you okay?"

Free at last from his sheets and blankets Dakota's tousled head appeared above the edge of his bed. "I was trying to skydive," he said.

Dakota's mom smiled at him, but he could see her brown eyes were worried. She was dressed in her SmartDollar uniform, a florescent orange and brown striped shirt that made her face look pale. Dakota wondered if his mom ever had anxiety dreams and, if she did, if she dreamed about that crazy uniform she had to wear.

"I need to leave for work now, honey," she said. "I'll be back for supper. How does pizza sound?"

"Great!" Next to chocolate sundaes and beef jerky, pizza was Dakota's favorite.

"Weren't you supposed to meet Shelly this morning?" his mom asked moving into his room and pulling open his curtains. Pale daylight swam into the chaos that was Dakota's bedroom. His mom sighed as the mess of clothes, books, model cars, posters and unmade bed was revealed.

"Not until 8:00," said Dakota. He scooped up his bedding from the floor and tossed it onto his bed. He tucked his memo book back under his pillow. His mom came over and gave him a bear hug. He hugged her back. *All in all she is a pretty good mom*, he thought.

"You'd better hurry, then," she said planting a kiss on the top of his head. "It's 7:45 now."

"Flying pterodactyls!" shouted Dakota borrowing

a phrase frequently used by PaleoJoe. "I've got to go!"

Dakota's mom smiled again as she watched her son turn into a miniature tornado of energy. "Be careful today," she said as Dakota careened out of the room.

"I will!" he shouted back, slamming the bathroom door.

Dakota's mom gathered up her purse and car keys and walked out the door. Her son would be only seconds behind her.

Throwing on some clothes and completely ignoring the fact that his hair was standing on end and needed to be combed, Dakota decided that he would never make his meeting with Shelly in time. It was going to be an important meeting too. Shelly had said she had a new case for the Dinosaur Detective Club. He was supposed to meet her on the steps of the Balboa Museum, which wasn't that far away from where he lived. But even though Dakota was a very fast runner, he knew he would never make it in time. He only had five minutes.

"It will have to be the board then," he muttered and diving into his closet he unearthed his skateboard. It was a long board, made for fast travel, and it was black decorated with a skull and flames.

The early morning sidewalks were mostly empty and Dakota went zooming along with no obstacles to slow him down. The cement burred under his wheels creating a rhythm of small, satisfying chunks as he

skimmed over the sidewalk cracks. He had to cross one intersection, but he timed it so perfectly that he got the walk light and sailed through without even stopping.

The air was cool and crisp. Dakota savored his speed.

"Whoohoo!" he yelled, swerving around Mrs. Trilby as she put coins in a parking meter.

And then there was the Balboa just ahead. He could see Shelly in her pink jacket already waiting on

the steps for him. He could also see that there was another girl with Shelly. He didn't know who it was, but he knew that Shelly would introduce him as soon as he got there.

But stopping proved to be a challenge.

"Hi, Shelllleeeeeee," yelled Dakota, meaning to come to a dramatic stop exactly next to her, but instead, when his skateboard hit the corner of the bottom museum step, the sudden, crashing jolt caused Dakota to dramatically fly off his board and go catapulting over the low chain that fenced off the grass from the sidewalk. He heard a squeal and a gasp as he went sailing by and then his chin plowed into the grass and the dewy moisture of the ground quickly soaked into the front of his shirt.

CHAPTER THREE

MR. DAREDEVIL

Two pink shoes pattered through the wet grass and came to a stop just by Dakota's nose.

"Hi, Shelly," said Dakota without looking up. He knew it was Shelly Brooks, because who else would be wearing pink shoes like those? "Your shoe is untied."

Puzzled, Shelly looked down at her neatly tied shoes. "No it isn't," she said.

Dakota reached out and quickly tweaked one of her laces effectively untying it. "Yes it is!"

"Dakota!" Shelly squealed dancing back, but by far, too late. "You pest!"

Annoyed, she crouched down to retie her shoe, trying to balance so she wouldn't have to kneel in the dewy grass. It was a bit tricky, but she managed it.

Dakota stood up and retrieved his skateboard,

which had landed upside down, its wheels spinning in the air, several feet away.

Shoe tied, skateboard retrieved, the two friends met up on the museum steps where the girl, who was unknown to Dakota, waited for them, clearly suppressing a fit of giggles.

"It's okay," Dakota told her. "Laugh if you want to."

"Dakota, you are such a brainless trilobite!" Shelly scowled at him. She noticed that he was quite a mess. There were muddy, smeary wet blotches on his jacket and jeans from his spectacular landing on the lawn and the tip of his chin was green where he had plowed into the grass. His hair, always weird anyway, was standing completely on end. And not, Shelly realized, because he had spiked it on purpose, but because he had not combed it at all.

Dakota grinned. "Just call me Mr. Daredevil!"

Unable to contain herself any longer, the girl burst out laughing. "You look like you grow a green beard on your chin!" she exclaimed.

A little embarrassed Dakota rubbed at his chin.

"He's an idiot," said Shelly, but she was laughing at him too. "Anyway, Mr. Daredevil, I would like you meet my friend Sarra Fenniche."

Shelly thought her friend had a beautiful name. *Sarra* had the same sound as the words *far* and *star.*

"Sarra is from Morocco," Shelly explained. "Her mom is my French teacher. Sarra, this is Dakota Jackson."

"Nice to meet you," said Sarra, her dark eyes still twinkling with laughter. Her voice was soft and musical, as though she had some kind of accent. She was carrying a large blue bag slung over her shoulder and she had short, curly hair that bounced when she laughed.

"Hi," said Dakota.

"Sarra has a mystery for PaleoJoe to solve," Shelly explained. "That's why I asked you to meet us here."

"Great!" said Dakota, suddenly feeling excited about the prospect of another mystery. Also, he realized, now he could put off telling Shelly about the essay contest until PaleoJoe had heard about Sarra's mystery and maybe even longer if Dakota could come up with more excuses.

"What are we waiting for? Let's go!"

With Shelly hot on his heels and Sarra not too far behind, Mr. Daredevil led the charge up the museum steps. But, as the trio bolted through the front doors, they collided with a woman carrying an armload of books.

"Oof!" said Dakota inventing impressive contortions as he bent and twisted trying to catch the falling books.

"Ow!" said Shelly who had crashed into Dakota, tripped over his big feet, and landed hard on her backside.

"Oh my!" said the woman as she lost her armload

of books and reeled back, arms whirling like a windmill, from the missile-like impact of the three children. Or rather from the impact of two children because Sarra, a little behind Shelly and Dakota, had been able to avoid disaster by stopping in time. Now she stood wide-eyed at the confusion in front of her, feeling very much in danger of another giggle attack.

But it wouldn't be polite to laugh, she thought. Still, Shelly sprawled on the floor, and Dakota's strange gyrations, and the grimace on the face of the woman were all very funny. Quickly, Sarra swallowed a laugh, which turned into a hiccup.

Always out and about with her arms full of books, the woman Shelly and Dakota had toppled into was Gamma Brooks.

"Mr. Daredevil strikes again," said Shelly, with an angry look at Dakota.

"Shelly Brooks!" said Gamma shaking her head at her granddaughter. "What were you thinking?"

Annoyed, Shelly scrambled to her feet. It was typical of Dakota to get her into trouble like this. The boy was a walking disaster zone.

"I'm sorry, Gamma," she apologized.

"It was my fault, Mrs. Brooks," said Dakota picking up the scattered books. "I wasn't looking where I was going."

"Apology accepted—this time," said Gamma Brooks looking over the tops of her glasses at Dakota as he handed her the books. Why was this boy always so scuffed and muddy? She shook her head. Gamma Brooks thought she would like to get him into a bathtub and give him a good scrubbing. She turned to Shelly. "You better get going, Little Pumpernickel. PaleoJoe is waiting for you."

"Thanks, Gamma. See you later!" said Shelly. Currently she was staying with her Gamma Brooks for about a week, while her parents were out of town.

"What is pumpernickel?" asked Sarra as the three made their way, walking now, to the stairwell.

"It's a kind of bread," said Shelly.

"Your grandmother calls you a kind of bread?" Sarra was puzzled.

"It's a long story," said Shelly. "Come on! We've got to enter the Tombs!"

CHAPTER FOUR

PANIC IN THE TOMBS

The children descended the big, creaky staircase that led to the basement of the Balboa. Both Shelly and Dakota loved the squeakiness of these ancient stairs and the way the sounds seemed to follow you as you marched down the polished length of them.

"Where are we going?" Sarra asked and her voice echoed weirdly in the stairwell.

"It's called The Tombs," said Shelly. "It's the basement of the museum. Hardly anyone gets to go down here and it's closed off to visitors. This is where PaleoJoe has his office. You'll see!"

"Hey, Sarra, check this out," said Dakota and he did a little dance jig on stairs seven and eight, two of the stairs with the best squeakability.

Squeeekee, squeak, crikki, crakkee swik creak!

"Do you recognize it?" And Dakota did it again, only a little faster this time.

"Hear what?" demanded Shelly. "You're just making a lot of *squwiks* and *criks*. Cool, but totally meaningless."

"Meaningless? I'll have you know I'm making serious music here. Listen!" With his skateboard banging a rhythm against his knee, Dakota hopped on his chosen stairs once again.

Squeeekee, squeak, crikki, crakkee swik creak!

Sarra and Shelly looked blankly at each other.

"Oh come on! Don't you recognize it? It's *Yellow Submarine.*"

"Who would recognize that?" Shelly rolled her eyes. "Maybe some tone deaf spiders or dancing cockroaches, but not anyone else!"

"Or beetles?" Dakota gave Sarra a mischievous grin, cracking up at his own joke. Sarra looked nervously down at her shoes. She didn't know what to make of Dakota yet.

"Come on, Dakota." Shelly was impatient. "We're late!"

Dakota shrugged and, maybe just to show off a little, he jumped the last three stairs and landed at the locked door a bit ahead of the two girls.

"Now what?" asked Sarra. She pulled her blue bag a little tighter against her side. Dakota wondered what she had in it. Books? It was sort of a big bag. It bulged oddly here and there as though it held something shaped very strangely. "That sign on the door says 'No admittance.' Doesn't that mean we can't get in?"

Dakota and Shelly looked at each other and grinned. This was all part of the adventure and they loved every minute of it.

Shelly knocked at the door. *Rap- a tat- a -tattat-rap-rap*. It was the new, specially coded knock. Dakota thought it had a great rhythm. He did a little dance step to the beat.

Slowly the door creaked open and a large man with a great black beard appeared in the doorway. Sarra looked a little nervously at this large figure. He did appear sort of menacing. Dakota noticed that she looked concerned and flashed her a grin of reassurance. This was Bob, the Maintenance Chief. Dakota always thought he looked like a pirate, a little nefarious, and maybe a little dangerous, too.

"Who dares to enter the Tombs?" Bob's voice boomed. He sounded like a pirate too.

"We do!" shouted Shelly and Dakota together.

Sarra clutched her blue bag closer, looked nervously back at the stairs, and thought about escape.

"Brave Explorers, in order to gain entrance to the Tombs," boomed Bob, "you must first answer a question."

Shelly looked sharply at Dakota. Whatever the question was, she intended to answer it first. She grinned thinking how foolish Dakota would look when he couldn't answer as fast as she could.

Dakota looked at Shelly. He could see that Miss-Know-It-All look in her eye. It drove him crazy when she got like that!

But, as it turned out, Bob never got to ask his question, because just then someone began shouting.

"Help! Help!" The shout came echoing down the long hallway. "Come quickly! Somebody help!"

CHAPTER FIVE

TERRIBLE TEETH

Dakota and Shelly pushed past Bob and pelted full speed down the long hallway. They had recognized the voice. They knew who was in trouble.

A flapping, dancing figure appeared in a doorway clear at the end of the hallway. "Mastodon Molars! Somebody help me!"

It was PaleoJoe.

"What is it, PaleoJoe?" asked Shelly. "What's wrong?"

"Quick, get the acetone! I've glued my fingers together!" PaleoJoe flapped his hand in her face and now Dakota and Shelly could see that his big thumb was sealed tightly to his index finger.

"Calm down," Shelly instructed, taking charge. "And stop hopping about like a giant grasshopper!

Quick, Dakota, the acetone is under the sink over there."

Dakota, trying hard not to laugh, dived into the clutter and chaos that was PaleoJoe's office and made his way to a small brown cabinet, mostly buried under piles of books, a box of bones, and what looked like a large roll of brown paper on a stick, but turned out to be an old wasp's nest. When he opened the door, he easily spotted the bottle of acetone next to a raggy, orange towel. He grabbed both the bottle and the towel.

Meanwhile Shelly had persuaded PaleoJoe to sit down. He teetered on the edge of a rickety stool and his face was a bright red. His eyes were watering a little from the small pain of trying to pry his fingers apart.

"Brontosaurus livers!" he grumbled, as Dakota gave Shelly the bottle of acetone and she began soaking a corner of the raggy towel with it. "I looked all over the place for that bottle. Thought they were going to have to cut my fingers off this time!"

A small gasp from the doorway alerted PaleoJoe to Sarra. He saw her eyes open very wide at the mention of fingers being cut off. Gruffly he cleared his throat. "Well, maybe I'm exaggerating just a bit," he said. Wouldn't be a good idea, he thought, to scare Shelly's new friend before he actually met her.

"Not only are you exaggerating, PaleoJoe, but you know full well that *brontosaurus* is not the correct name to use if you want to be scientifically accurate," said Shelly shaking her head.

"I wasn't being scientific," grumbled PaleoJoe. "I was being disgruntled."

"Cool word," said Dakota. "Does that have anything to do with pigs?"

"Of course it doesn't," said Shelly, in her superior sort of way. "Now hold still!" She dabbed the moistened towel on PaleoJoe's stuck-together fingers. "It won't take me long to get your fingers apart if you'll stop jittering and flapping about and let me work!"

"Everything under control then, PaleoJoe?" asked Bob leaning in the doorway peering over the top of Sarra's head. Dakota noticed how he was looking over PaleoJoe's office, as though he were trying to memorize what he saw. *It is a strange office,* thought Dakota. Maybe Bob did not clean in here and was curious about it.

"Yes, thanks Bob," said PaleoJoe, trying to sit still for Shelly, and Bob disappeared to return to his work as maintenance chief.

"Nice," said Dakota grinning. "I guess we got in today without answering a question."

Shelly scowled, remembering how she was planning on being the first to answer Bob's question. "PaleoJoe," she with irritation, "how did you manage to do this?"

"I was trying to glue a *Titanothere* tooth back together." He gestured to his desk where a broken bone lay in pieces under a pool of light from the powerful lamp PaleoJoe used when he was doing delicate work

on fossils.

"A titanno-whatsit?" asked Dakota.

"A *Titanothere* was a primitive Rhinoceros that lived on the central plains of the United States about 10 million years ago," said PaleoJoe.

Dakota went over to the desk to examine PaleoJoe's project. "Wow," he said. "It looks like a jigsaw puzzle."

"There you are!" exclaimed Shelly triumphantly as PaleoJoe's fingers finally came apart.

"You're a genius, Miss Shelly Brooks," laughed PaleoJoe and he snapped his fingers to prove it.

"You're welcome," said Shelly. She put the cap back on the bottle and returned both bottle and towel to their place under the cabinet. She knew that sometime they would be needed again.

"So, Shelly, is this your friend from Morocco?" asked PaleoJoe.

"Yes. PaleoJoe, this is my friend Sarra Fenniche. Sarra has a mystery for you!"

"Oh good," said PaleoJoe. "I love mysteries."

Sarra smiled. She liked PaleoJoe's friendly blue eyes. Dressed in olive green pants with the khaki sleeves of his shirt rolled over his elbows, he looked like he was ready for an expedition. His short, carefully trimmed graying beard made him look wise. Shelly had told Sarra a lot about her friend and now, after meeting him, Sarra was sure he would be able to help her.

"Ah, Morocco!" PaleoJoe dreamily leaned back

in his chair. "Land of adventure, danger and deserts, mountains, treasure and some really cool trilobite fossils–a great and wonderful place of stories."

"Have you been there?" asked Dakota intrigued.

"Once," said PaleoJoe. "Here, let me show you something."

Shelly, Dakota, and Sarra crowded close behind PaleoJoe as he went over to his desk where, pinned to the wall just under the narrow rectangle of an open window, was a giant world map.

"Look. Here is Morocco," he said pointing to an area towards the top of the bulgy side of the African continent. "It's on the coast of North Africa."

"And this is where I lived," said Sarra excitedly pinpointing the city of Casablanca.

"Casablanca is the largest city in Morocco," said PaleoJoe. "It's a very important port for ships and trade as well."

"Yes," said Sarra. "My grandfather used to take us to the docks to watch the big ships come in."

"Well," said PaleoJoe settling himself in his chair. "Let's hear about this mystery of yours."

"Okay," said Sarra. "It has to do with these."

And from her blue, canvas bag Sarra pulled out two of the biggest, curved, knife-like teeth Dakota had ever seen in his life.

CHAPTER SIX

SARRA'S STORY

PaleoJoe whistled like a teapot full of steam. "*Smilodon* teeth!"

"*Smilodon* teeth?" asked Shelly clearly very impressed. "Is that what these are, PaleoJoe?"

"Without a doubt," said PaleoJoe carefully cradling one of the dagger-like teeth in the palm of his hand. "*Smilodon fatalis*."

"So what you're saying is that some guy named Don has really big teeth and smiles a lot," joked Dakota. "Get it? Smile - O - Don?

But his joke fell flat.

"For your information," said Shelly in her superior I-know-it-all tone of voice, "we are talking about saber-toothed tigers, here."

"Well, they weren't actually tigers," PaleoJoe

corrected her. Shelly saw Dakota smirk and she felt her face get warm. Of course she knew that, she had just been so excited and forgot. "Sabertooths are really from the cat family. But they had short tails, like bobcats. Still, they were giant cats by any measure and then they had these really big canine teeth." PaleoJoe traced his finger along the curve of the tooth he held. "This tooth here is a good 9 inches long."

"They look like curved knives," observed Dakota.

"Yes," PaleoJoe agreed. "*Smilodon* means 'knife-tooth.' And, for that matter, a saber is also a type of curved sword. "

"Awesomeness," said Dakota very impressed.

"Where did you get these, Sarra?" asked PaleoJoe.

"That's the mystery, PaleoJoe," said Shelly jumping in. "Go on, Sarra, tell him. Don't leave anything out. Don't forget about the cardboard box and Phoenix, and the safe and the strange man who came to dinner and how he smelled like camels and also don't forget about the...*ulp*"

PaleoJoe clamped a hand on Shelly's shoulder cutting her off. "Sit," he said raising an eyebrow at her, a trick Dakota greatly admired. "Zip and listen."

So Shelly settled herself on one of the stools. Dakota perched on the edge of PaleoJoe's desk. PaleoJoe leaned back in his chair with a pencil and pad of paper handy in case he had to make notes, and Sarra began her story.

"It was two weeks before my 9th birthday," said Sarra in her softly accented voice. "My mother and brother and I lived in a nice apartment in Casablanca. My brother, Amine, is many years older than I am and he is working with my Grandfather in his shop of gifts. Our apartment is close to this shop and it is easy for my brother to get to work.

"Amine is always giving me special gifts from Grandfather's shop every birthday time. He always surprises me."

"Tell about the nestled dolls, the matrioshka" said Shelly unable, of course, to remain completely out of the story.

Sarra smiled at her friend. She had shown Shelly the nestled dolls and knew they were one of Shelly's favorites. "Once Amine gave me a matrioshka for my birthday time. It is a wooden doll made in Russia, but it has a secret. It looks like it is one, fat, round doll with pink painted cheeks. But she is really a box and if you open her up there is another doll inside her with a green scarf and red cheeks. She, too, is a box and when you open her up there is another, smaller doll inside her too. There are five dolls all nestled together. The last one is a baby painted very pretty and smiling."

"Smiling-Donna," said Dakota. No one laughed.

"Go on," said PaleoJoe. "How did you get the fossils?"

"So two weeks before my birthday time, my brother Amine comes home one afternoon. My mother is out and only I am at home, but my brother does not know this. From my bedroom window I see him come in and he is carrying a big box. I think that this might be my birthday present. I spy on him as he comes upstairs with the box and I watch him take it into his room. I can hear by the movement he makes, that he is putting the box under his bed.

"Then, my brother, he leaves the apartment. I decide I will go and peek in the box and see what he has bought for my birthday gift."

"Present-spying!" said Dakota knowingly. "Do it all the time. Mom has nowhere she can hide a present

that I won't find it."

"Great," said Shelly. "Now you are bragging about your dishonesty. What do you want, a medal?"

"Hey," said Dakota. "Present-spying is an art form. Just because you get caught when you do it."

"I do not get caught!" Shelly flared at him.

"Aha!" said Dakota shaking a finger in her face. "So you admit to present-spying!"

Infuriated, Shelly looked around for something to throw at him. The only thing to hand her were Sarra's fossils. No good throwing those. She settled for insult instead. "*Trachodon* face!"

Dakota looked at PaleoJoe. "Duck-billed dinosaur," PaleoJoe informed Dakota and studied the eraser end of the pencil he held as though it were of great importance.

Smugly, Shelly smirked. Dakota stuck his tongue out at her, which did, in fact, make him look a little like *Trachodon*. Sarra looked bewildered.

"Ignore them," advised PaleoJoe. "Please continue your story, Sarra."

"Well, my brother hides the box under his bed and then he leaves the apartment. I sneak into his room and I find the box under his bed just as I think. I pull it out and when I look inside I see it is full of old bones."

"What did they look like?" asked PaleoJoe clearly very interested.

"Two of the bones are these," said Sarra pointing

to the teeth. “And the other is a skull of some animal. Here, I make a sketch of it for you.”

Sarra dug in her back pocket and pulled out a folded piece of paper, which she handed to PaleoJoe. Eagerly he unfolded it and looked wide-eyed at Sarra’s sketch.

“Iguanodon toenails,” breathed PaleoJoe in excitement. “A saber-toothed skull! Or, at least, it’s a good possibility it was. But was this the way it looked, Sarra?”

“What do you mean?” Sarra was puzzled. “That is the way I saw it.”

“Hmmmm,” PaleoJoe stroked his beard.

“What is it, PaleoJoe?” asked Shelly.

“Well, if this is the skull Sarra saw then it might be a very special skull indeed. You see the saber-toothed cat skulls that have been discovered have always been found with their mouth open. This one appears to have its mouth closed. This is a very good sketch, Sarra.”

“Thank-you,” said Sarra. “Yes, I think that it was the great cat’s skull, too and I remember that the mouth was closed when I picked it up.”

“That is very interesting,” said PaleoJoe. “What happened next?”

“I put the skull back in the box. Then I took the teeth out of the box and I was looking at them when unexpectedly, my brother returns. I don’t have time to put the teeth back so I shove the box under the bed and hide the teeth under my shirt and rush into my own room. My brother does not hear me and I think that I will return the teeth later when he goes out again. But he goes into his bedroom and he gets the box from under his bed. He gets it quickly and he does not look in it so he does not know that the teeth are missing. And then he leaves the apartment. From my bedroom window I see him get into his car and he drives away.

"PaleoJoe, I need your help," said Sarra, "because when my brother gets in his car and drives away we never see him again."

CHAPTER SEVEN

THE MOST DEADLY PLACE ON EARTH

"Well, this is very interesting," said PaleoJoe. "You said this was just before your 9th birthday?"

Sarra nodded.

"That would mean that your brother has been missing for two years!" PaleoJoe shook his head. "I think you want a detective, Sarra, not a paleontologist."

"But that isn't all of her story, PaleoJoe," said Shelly. "There's more!"

"Okay," said PaleoJoe. "I'll hear the rest."

"When my brother did not return, my mother gets very concerned. She is worried all the time anyway because my grandfather was very sick and in the hospital. Now with my brother disappeared, she

was very afraid.

"About a week after my brother is gone, Mr. Salah, my grandfather's partner, comes to my mother and accuses my brother of stealing something valuable from the safe in the gift store. What was in the safe, my mother asks him? He does not know, but he knows that it is gone.

"Mother talks with Grandfather. He tells my mother that Amine is doing something important my grandfather has asked him to do. Grandfather tells my mother that what was in the safe was his and he gave it to Amine to take care of."

"So what was it? In the safe, I mean," asked Dakota.

Sarra shrugged. "Grandfather would not say."

"I bet it was the Sabertooth fossils," said Dakota.

"Tell about the strange man who came to supper," urged Shelly.

"On my birthday, Mr. Salah is invited to dinner. It is a tradition that he always comes on my birthday, but usually Grandfather is there, too. But Grandfather is more sick and cannot leave the hospital so Mr. Salah comes and brings a friend with him.

"Mr. Salah says his friend is an expert in fossils. He says that the contents of Grandfather's safe were valuable fossils and Amine took them."

"I knew it!" yelled Dakota punching his fist in the air and almost falling off PaleoJoe's desk.

"Mr. Salah says that when Grandfather dies the shop will belong to him and so he wants Amine to return the fossils or he will have to report Amine as a thief," Sarra continued. "My mother is very upset and she asked Mr. Salah and his friend to leave."

"His friend smelled like camel feet," said Shelly watching to see if PaleoJoe made a note of that detail.

Sarra gave a sad smile. "That was what Mother said because she was mad. He did not really smell. My Grandfather died a few days after my birthday. Mr. Salah came again to ask about Amine, but Mother said we did not know where he was. Mr. Salah said he would have to report the theft of the fossils. Mother persuaded him to wait until she could find out what happened to my brother. Mr. Salah said he would wait only a little bit.

"I did not tell anyone I had these teeth. I did not want to risk getting Amine into more trouble. I was sure that when he discovered the teeth were gone from his box he would return to look for them.

"In the next month after my birthday we got a postcard from my brother. It was a birthday card for me, but it had become lost in the mail. It was from your Angel City. Amine said to tell Grandfather he was staying with Miss Phoenix and that he would do what Grandfather had asked of him before coming back home.

"Of course with Grandfather gone we could not ask him who was Miss Phoenix, and Amine did

not give us an address and so we could not tell him of Grandfather's passing."

"And so Sarra and her mom came to America to live with an uncle while Sarra's mom teaches French to try and make enough money to hire a private detective to find Sarra's brother," said Shelly power summarizing the end of the story.

"But what about that Salah guy and Camel Feet?" asked Dakota. "Did they report Amine as a thief?"

Sarra shook her head. "No. Mr. Salah sold the shop and never said anything more about it. His friend we never saw again."

PaleoJoe opened his mouth to ask Sarra a question but he wasn't fast enough. Dakota, who wanted to grow up to be a detective, was faster.

"Where is this Angel City you said Amine wrote from?" Dakota demanded.

"My guess would be Los Angeles," said PaleoJoe. And then, before Dakota could interrupt, he continued. "And a smart person would now ask me why I think that. And I would answer I think that because of these teeth."

He picked up one of the Sabertooth canines and held it under the desk light. The tooth was an amber brown color like ancient earth. "This canine is clearly from the La Brea Tar Pits," he said enjoying the surprised looks of the kids. "And the tar pits were one of the deadliest places on earth for saber-toothed cats."

CHAPTER EIGHT

A FOSSIL SPEAKS

"I do know a thing or two," said PaleoJoe smiling at the drop-jawed look of Shelly and Dakota. "After all, I am the Dinosaur Detective, right?"

"How do you know these fossils came from there?" asked Shelly.

"A fossil can tell you many things if you know how to listen and fossils from La Brea are unique," said PaleoJoe. "Most fossils have been turned to stone or altered or changed in some way, like the outline of a leaf left in a rock. But the bones from La Brea are still bones because they have been preserved by asphalt. They are this dark coffee color because of the asphalt. Bones are porous and as they lay in the asphalt they became saturated with the oil. The oil pushed all air and oxygen out of them and prevented them from

decaying."

"Perfectly preserved," said Shelly amazed.

"But why is La Brea deadly? asked Dakota.

"Rancho La Brea is Spanish for *tar ranch.* It is one of the richest and most famous asphalt deposits of Ice Age fossils in the world," said PaleoJoe. "Many animals got trapped in the tar and perished."

"A tomb of tar," said Dakota scowling and lowering his voice dramatically. He thought he sounded a bit like Bob.

"In a way," said PaleoJoe. "You remember that book I lent to you awhile back, Dakota?"

Dakota knew very well what book PaleoJoe was talking about, but this was dangerous ground. He had borrowed the book to research his topic of Dire Wolves for the essay contest. Now, if only PaleoJoe would *not* bring *that* up! "Um, the one about the Dire Wolves?" said Dakota.

"Exactly. The most common fossils dug up out of the Tar Pits belong to Dire Wolves and, California's state fossil, the saber-toothed cat."

"Wow," said Shelly, her eyes shining. "I can't imagine what that must be like to dig in tar and to find all those fossils."

"It's very amazing," said PaleoJoe.

"So you think Amine might be in this Los Angeles city?" asked Sarra.

"Trapped in the tar pits?" asked Dakota eagerly.

"No, not trapped in the tar pits," said PaleoJoe.

"Although asphalt seeps do still trap things from time to time. Even people. But what I meant was that Sarra's brother could possibly be in Los Angeles. I still think you need a different kind of detective to find him. But there is no doubt that this fossil," and he patted one of the teeth, "came from La Brea. And I will tell you something else about these fossils of yours, Sarra. I think one of them is a fake."

"A fake!" Shelly squealed. "How do you know that?"

"Well, I don't," said PaleoJoe. "Not for sure. But there is a way I can find out. Is that okay with you, Sarra?"

"Of course," said Sarra.

"Dakota, in that drawer over there, you will find a candle. Get it for us, please," directed PaleoJoe. "Shelly, look in my coat pocket behind the door for a box of matches."

Dakota and Shelly did as directed, each finding the requested item. "Now," said PaleoJoe lighting the candle, "Shelly, in my tool roll you'll find a pin."

"I'm on it!" said Shelly diving for a low cupboard on the far side of the room. All but disappearing inside it, she somehow managed to retrieve PaleoJoe's tool roll.

Carefully, PaleoJoe unrolled the canvas carrier of his paleontology tools. Shelly watched, grinning. She now had her very own tool roll and she loved the neatly organized set of tools that were revealed. From

amongst the small chisels and trowels and brushes, PaleoJoe extracted a common pin.

"I didn't know you had that in there," said Shelly, thinking she would have to remember to put one into her own roll.

"This is a very important tool," said PaleoJoe mysteriously. Using a pair of tweezers, he held the pin over the candle flame until the point became very hot.

"Why do people fake fossils?" Sarra asked as she watched these preparations.

"Well," said PaleoJoe. "There is a lot of dishonest money to be made on black market fossils. Some of the black market fossils are stolen and quite a number of them are faked. Unwary collectors can spend a great deal of money and never even know they have been fooled."

"So you can tell a fake fossil by sticking a pin in it?" asked Dakota. He had taken another small note pad from his hip pocket. Unlike the blue one under his pillow, this one was black. It was his Detective Notebook. In it he was carefully writing down this procedure to determine a fake fossil. Dakota figured that if paleontologists needed tool rolls to do their work, detectives needed notebooks.

"Some fake fossils can be determined like this," said PaleoJoe. "Some are so well done that the only way to really tell is to destroy them."

"What good is that?" Shelly demanded. "What if it isn't a fake, then what?"

"Then you have destroyed a perfectly good fossil," said PaleoJoe. "But we won't have to do that to this tooth. Sometimes people fake bones by using an acrylic or plastic mixed with other substances to make the bone. So, let's just see."

PaleoJoe placed the tip of the now red-hot pin gently on the side of the tooth he thought was a fake. Wide-eyed Shelly, Dakota, and Sarra watched as the pin tip melted into the bone and a faint smell of burning plastic tickled their noses.

"Yep," said PaleoJoe. "It's a fake. The hot needle melts the plastic and you can smell it burning."

"What happens to people who fake fossils?" asked Sarra, a sudden feeling of fear rising in her stomach.

"Faking fossils and selling them on the black market is a very serious crime," said PaleoJoe. "If someone is caught doing that, they go to jail!"

CHAPTER NINE

WHO IS SMARTER?

A little bit later, Shelly, Dakota and Sarra left PaleoJoe's office. They gathered outside the museum on the front steps to talk over what they had discovered.

PaleoJoe said that he would speak to Detective Franks about Sarra's missing brother, but that there was little else he could do.

"Detective Franks knows his stuff," said Dakota trying to reassure Sarra. "I'm sure he'll think of something."

PaleoJoe had told Sarra to keep her fossils safe because the Sabertooth canine that wasn't a fake was valuable. Someday she may want to let a museum put it on display.

"I don't know," said Shelly. "I thought that PaleoJoe could do more to help you, Sarra."

"It's okay," said Sarra in her soft voice. "I know more now then I did before."

"That's true," said Dakota. "Now we know that your brother is probably in Los Angeles."

"Is that very far away?" asked Sarra.

"It's practically on the other side of the continent," said Shelly gloomily.

"Would it be hard to get there? You see, I just think that if I could go there I could find Amine," said Sarra.

"It would be really hard," said Shelly.

"No it wouldn't," said Dakota. "It would be a piece of cake if you flew."

And then he thought about kicking himself in the head. Why was he so stupid sometimes?

"That's right!" said Shelly excitedly going exactly where Dakota had been hoping she wouldn't go. "And I know a way we can there, Sarra!"

"How?" asked Sarra eagerness making her eyes sparkle.

"You see, there is this essay contest that I entered," said Shelly.

"We entered," said Dakota. "I wrote an essay too, remember."

"Yes," said Shelly brushing off Dakota's interruption. "But if I win it, I get free airline tickets. I should be hearing any day now and I know I'm going to win it!"

"But how do you know you will win?" asked Sarra.

"Oh, because I will," said Shelly confidently. "I wrote about Dinosaur Sue and I know all about that dinosaur. PaleoJoe and I solved a very complicated case about it when it was stolen from the museum. Oh, sorry, Dakota," Shelly, caught up in her own enthusiasm, suddenly noticed the look on Dakota's face. "Dakota's essay was pretty good, too," she said to Sarra but Dakota thought it sounded like one of those empty compliments your teachers make to your mom when they don't want to tell the truth about how badly you are really doing in class.

"How do you know that he won't win?" Sarra asked.

There was an uncomfortable silence and then Shelly laughed. "Because everyone knows I'm smarter than he is," she said. "And besides, Dakota never wins anything. He's a terrible student and spends most of his time in trouble in the principal's office. I'm sorry, Dakota, but it's the truth."

It might have been the truth, but she shouldn't have said it out loud and not in front of Sarra because Dakota's feelings were suddenly and terribly hurt. And that made him mad.

"Oh yeah," he said, anger turning his face red. His uncombed hair standing straight up in the air seemed charged with fury. "That just shows how much you know about it because I DID win the essay contest. They chose MY essay about the Dire Wolves over your stupid essay on Dinosaur Sue."

Shelly felt an answering anger building up inside her. Dakota was always such an idiot, she thought. And he was a liar, too.

"You're a liar!" she shouted. And now both Dakota and Shelly were standing on the museum steps nose to nose shouting at each other. Sarra stood to one side feeling very embarrassed.

"I am not a liar," said Dakota furiously and reaching into his pocket he pulled out the letter and shook it in Shelly's face. "See for yourself!"

Shelly ripped the letter from Dakota's hand and tore it open. The letter, which Dakota knew by heart, went like this:

Dear Mr. Jackson,

Cross Continental Airlines is pleased to inform you that you have won first place in the Junior Paleontology Essay Contest for your essay entitled **Dire Wolves of the Ice Age.** Please find enclosed your two free, first class airline tickets for any destination within the continental United States.

Congratulations and good luck with future essay contests.

Yours Very Truly,
Alvin Conrad,
CEO Cross Continental Airlines

As she read the letter, Shelly's face went a bright red and then very pale.

"Dakota, I hate you!" she yelled as she finished. Shelly threw the letter on the ground and, turning away, she sprinted down the sidewalk.

Sarra, stunned by the outburst, let her go. Shelly was a fast runner and Sarra would not be able to catch up with her anyway. Wide-eyed Sarra looked at Dakota who stood for a moment, shoulders slumped as though all the air had been let out of him. He watched Shelly disappear down the street.

Slowly, Dakota bent to retrieve his letter. Carefully he folded it up and put it back in his pocket. All anger had vanished leaving him feeling numb and empty. He wasn't mad at Shelly anymore. How could he be? He had seen the heartbreak, bewilderment and the tears forming in the corner of her eyes as she read the letter.

CHAPTER TEN

DANGER IS CLOSE

"Oh well, it doesn't matter, Sarra," said Dakota. "You can still have the airline tickets to go find your brother."

"No," said Sarra. "Thank you Dakota, but I could not use your tickets. My mother and I will find another way. Now I must hurry or I will miss my bus."

"Come on, follow me," said Dakota. "I know a short cut to the bus stop."

Glumly he led Sarra around the corner of the Balboa and down a narrow alley that ran alongside the building. The alleyway sloped down and soon Dakota and Sarra found themselves opposite a partially open basement window.

"Hey," said Dakota with a sudden inspiration of something that would cheer him up. "That's PaleoJoe's

office window. Let's play a joke on him."

"Dakota, I don't think we should," Sarra protested, but Dakota, a Mr. Daredevil smile on his face, put his finger to his lips and shushed her.

Putting his back to the brick wall of the building he inched his way toward the open window. "I'm just going to do a little ghost wailing," Dakota whispered. "You see there is supposed to be a ghost that haunts this old museum. Let's just see what PaleoJoe thinks when he hears it!"

Dakota grinned evilly as he inched closer to the window. Sarra looked very nervous. She was wondering if there was any way she could just turn around and leave when she heard voices coming from the open window. She felt her heart freeze as she heard what was being said.

"I think it sounds like a case of fossil smuggling, Franks," said PaleoJoe.

Cautiously, Dakota peered into the half open window. PaleoJoe sat at his desk just below the window, the phone held to his ear. Dakota knew that it was Detective Franks who was on the other end. Dakota and Sarra could hear every word PaleoJoe said.

PaleoJoe listened and then he said, "Yes, I agree with you and faking fossils is a serious crime. We need to do everything we can to bring the criminals to justice." He batted at a fly that buzzed around his head as he continued to listen. "Sure. Sure. But if you have to arrest someone..."

PaleoJoe picked up a rolled newspaper and swatted at the fly, which now appeared to be joined by two more.

"Franks, hold on just a minute, will you? I've got to close my window. I'm being invaded by flies!"

Sarra and Dakota flattened themselves back against the wall as PaleoJoe got up to close his window. He didn't see them but now, with the window closed, the rest of his conversation was just so much mumbling.

"Come on, Sarra," said Dakota. "Let's get out of here."

And running, he led her through the rest of the shortcut. They didn't stop until they reached the bus stop. Dakota bent over to catch his breath. Beside him Sarra was gulping air as well.

"Dakota, are they going to arrest me?" She gasped her eyes wide and frightened. "Do they think I'm smuggling fake fossils?

"I don't know," Dakota was clearly worried. He trusted PaleoJoe, but what they had heard definitely didn't sound good. "We need to talk to Shelly about this."

"I'm really scared," said Sarra. "Will the police just come and take me away?"

"No," said Dakota. "They don't do things like that."

"But they might." Sarra was frightened. "What if I go home and the police are there waiting for me?"

Dakota was starting to feel her panic. "Then you

can't go home," he said. "Look, I've got a plan. Let's go to Shelly's. She's staying with Gamma Brooks. Shelly will help us figure out what to do."

"Do you think she will talk to you?" asked Sarra. "She was very upset."

"She'll talk to me," said Dakota smiling a little bit to himself. "She really is, after all, smarter than me. She'll figure it out. Come on. It'll be faster on my board."

Sarra balanced on the back of Dakota's skateboard and held onto his belt loops. Going slower than his earlier rocket ride to the museum, but still going faster than walking, Dakota and Sarra zoomed their way to Shelly.

CHAPTER ELEVEN

TRUCE

Shelly ran into her Gamma Brook's apartment slamming the door behind her. She was grateful that her grandmother was still at the museum and wouldn't be home for hours yet. Shelly had stopped crying sometime on the bus ride home, but she still felt an angry clenching in her stomach.

There was only one way Dakota won that contest, Shelly thought as she stomped around the empty apartment.

He had cheated.

She didn't know how he had managed it, but she was sure that somehow he had. She thumped a pile of books off the sofa onto the floor. He had been so smug about it and then to tell her in front of Sarra like that! Oh, it was unbearable! She stamped her foot on the floor.

In the apartment below her, Mrs. Roberts had had enough of the thumps and bumps coming from upstairs. All that noise was interrupting her afternoon soaps. She took her broom and thumped the handle against the ceiling.

Shelly stuck her tongue out at the floor. She knew Mrs. Roberts and thought she was an old busy body. The woman was always complaining about something. But she didn't want to get Gamma Brooks in trouble so she threw herself down on the sofa for a good sulk.

Below her Mrs. Roberts went back to watching her T.V. and, except for that thundercloud of a frown on Shelly's face, all seemed peaceful.

When I find out how that idiot cheated, she thought her chin on her fist, *I'm going to rat him out but good and make sure he gives the tickets back to that airline.*

She rested her head back on the blue flowered upholstery of Gamma's couch and began planning Dakota's downfall.

She was still there 20 minutes later when the doorbell buzzed.

Grumpily, Shelly went to the door and peered through the peephole that made the hallway beyond look like a fishbowl. It was Sarra. Shelly did not really want to see anyone but she couldn't be rude to Sarra.

She unlocked the door and opened it turning her back and walking back to the living room without looking at her friend.

"Come on in, Sarra," she said over her shoulder. "Shut the door, please."

Shelly threw herself on the couch and then she looked up to see not just Sarra standing in her living room, but Dakota Jackson as well.

Without even thinking about it, Shelly reached down for one of the books she had dumped on the floor and flung it at Dakota. The book, an historical account of the migratory patterns of the Monarch butterfly, swished toward Dakota's head, missed him by the

narrowest of margins, and thunked into the wall behind him.

Mrs. Roberts' broom handle angrily went tap-tap-tap. Shelly stamped her foot again just where she thought Mrs. Roberts might be standing. The broom tapping stopped.

"Dakota Jackson, I hate you and I'm not talking to you ever again. You can just get out!" exclaimed Shelly folding her arms and glaring at Dakota.

"Okay," said Dakota holding up his hands like they did in Westerns to show they were unarmed. It was supposed to keep you from getting killed by the guy shooting at you, but Dakota doubted, had Shelly been a Sheriff of the Old West, that he would have remained alive very long at all. "I'm not staying, but we have a serious problem, Shelly."

"Yes, we do," Shelly snapped at him. "You cheated on the contest and when I figure out how you did it, I'm going to tell everyone. You'll be in so much trouble you will never get out of it!"

Dakota had told himself that he would hold his temper no matter what Shelly said, but now he found himself getting angry anyway. "I did not cheat!" he said.

Quickly, Sarra stepped between the two and turned to face Shelly. "Shelly," she said urgently. "I need your help. The police are going to arrest me for faking fossils!"

"What?" Caught off guard by this announcement

Shelly felt her mouth gaping open. Quickly she closed it. “Is this some sort of joke Dakota cooked up, because if it is...”

“It isn’t,” said Dakota earnestly. “Please, Shelly. We need your help. Can’t we please just call a truce and help Sarra?”

Shelly looked from Dakota’s scowl, which made him look very dishonest, she thought, to Sarra’s face which clearly showed fright. There was something going on here and, by the looks of things, it was something serious.

“Okay,” said Shelly. “Truce for now, but this isn’t over yet, Dakota.”

Dakota nodded. It would give him some time to figure out how to convince Shelly he had won the contest fair and square.

Shelly sat up on the couch. “Have a seat and tell me what happened,” she said.

CHAPTER TWELVE

A PLAN OF ACTION

With Shelly thinking, it didn't take long to formulate a Plan of Action. And it was a very daring plan. Shelly felt most uneasy about it, but she didn't see any other way to help her friend. All three thought that the best solution to the problem was to find Sarra's brother, Amine, and to find him fast.

"I think he must be in Los Angeles," said Dakota using all the deductive reasoning he was capable of. "That's where the post card came from and that's where the La Brea Tar Pits are."

"You know, technically, when you say *The La Brea Tar Pits* you are actually saying *The The Tar Tar Pits*," Shelly observed.

"And that's important why?" asked Dakota thumping himself on the forehead.

"Okay. Good point," said Shelly. "Just thought

I'd mention it."

"Is Los Angeles a big city?" asked Sarra.

"Big enough," said Shelly. "We can't just roam up and down the streets calling your brother's name. Where would we begin to look for him?"

"Miss Phoenix," said Dakota the idea suddenly coming to him. "Let's try the Internet."

Shelly had booted up Gamma's computer and, with Dakota and Sarra hanging over her shoulder, she had launched into a genius Internet search for the lost Miss Phoenix.

And found her.

Dakota had to admire Shelly's ability. She was a whiz with technology. Dakota was lucky if he could turn a computer on.

Shelly found a woman by the name of Twila Phoenix who lived in Los Angeles, California.

"That has to be her," said Shelly squinting at the screen while Dakota scribbled notes in his memo book. "Here is her address and look, I can pull up a satellite image of her neighborhood."

"Wow," said Sarra. "It looks like we are flying above her house."

She was right. Shelly played around with the zoom and as Dakota watched, a bit uncomfortably, he was reminded about his nightmare.

"Which house is hers?" he asked.

"It looks like it's that sort of pinkish one at the end of that street," said Shelly.

"Too bad there isn't a telephone number, then we could just call her," said Dakota.

"Either she isn't listed or she doesn't have a phone," said Shelly. "There isn't any number."

"Then we'll just have to go visit her and ask her if she knows where Amine is," said Sarra sounding braver than she felt.

And that's how, about an hour later, Shelly found herself riding in a taxi to the airport on her first step toward Los Angeles. Because Sarra was afraid to go home for clothes, Shelly's pink backpack and Sarra's blue shoulder bag were bulging with weekend supplies for both of them.

"Let's just go over this once more to be sure we have it straight," said Shelly as they bumped through late afternoon traffic. The back of the taxi smelled musty and damp. Shelly was feeling decidedly nervous and a little car sick. Dishonesty might come naturally to Dakota, but she herself had real problems with it.

Dakota stifled a groan. How many times would they have to go over it, he wondered? Still, the truce was in effect and he would not argue with Shelly now.

What Shelly didn't know was that Dakota, too, felt very nervous about this plan. They could all get into a lot of trouble if they were caught. But it wasn't as though they were actually doing anything wrong, Dakota tried to argue with himself. *Oh, no. Nothing wrong. Just a little lying and flying across the country without permission. What was so wrong about that?*

Dakota sighed.

"As far as everyone knows," said Dakota keeping his voice low so they would not be overheard by the cabdriver, "you two are staying over at my house for the weekend working on designing some fossil exhibits for PaleoJoe."

Shelly nodded. She had called Gamma at the museum and it had been easy to get permission. Sarra also had no difficulty getting her mom to agree. They had decided on the fossil exhibit design as a cover story so that Dakota could tell his mom that they were spending their time at the museum.

"When you get to Los Angeles, you are going to try and find Sarra's brother." Dakota flipped open his black Detective's Notebook ticking off the details as he recited them. "I have your cell phone number in case I need to get hold of you. We have the secret coded signal, the Disaster Signal. I let the phone ring 2 rings and then hang up if anything goes wrong on my end."

"But nothing will," said Shelly noticing the nervous look on Sarra's face. "We will find your brother, Sarra, and be back before anyone knows we've been gone."

The taxi left them off at the airport. Shelly and Dakota had pooled all their allowance money and Dakota had given Shelly his tickets. She had taken them without looking at him. Still, the sacrifice of the tickets was to help Sarra, and Dakota actually felt good about that.

Dakota watched as Shelly and Sarra boarded a Cross Continental plane. He watched for a long time until he could no longer see Shelly's pink backpack in the crowd. And even then he didn't leave. He stood at the big airport observation windows and watched until the plane carrying his friends launched into the late afternoon sky. Only then did Dakota turn around to head home to pizza and the long weekend of keeping important secrets.

CHAPTER THIRTEEN

MR. BYRD

"2314 Orange Terrace," Shelly told the cab driver as she and Sarra clambered into the back seat of the taxi.

"No problem, little birdlets," said their cab driver. He was a very large, heavyset man who took up almost the entire front seat. He wore a dark green cap slanted over one eyebrow and he winked at the girls in the rearview mirror as he pulled away from the curb into the busy traffic flowing in and out of the Los Angeles airport. Then, putting on a very dark pair of sunglasses he began to sing something in Italian.

Sarra and Shelly looked at each other. It was about 3:00 in the afternoon, two hours earlier than at home. Not only were they in a different time zone, but also they were in a different state. It was weird.

Outside the taxi palm trees lined the roadways. The afternoon sun was very bright. Shelly rolled down her window a crack and the warm air that pushed into the cab was strangely scented.

"O Solo Mio," sang the cab driver a little off key and very loudly.

"I'm going to call Dakota," said Shelly. "I just want to check on things."

From her backpack she extracted her pink, space age cell phone. She had Dakota on speed dial. He answered on the third ring.

"What's going on?" he asked. "You sound like you're at a bullfight or something." Dakota did not actually know what it would sound like to be at a bullfight, but the strange noises he could hear in the background made him think about bulls.

"It's the cab driver," said Shelly. "He's singing."

"How was the flight?" Dakota thought Shelly sounded nervous, but he was glad she wasn't, at the moment, yelling at him. "Did anyone follow you?"

"The flight was great. If someone was following us we couldn't tell. I just wanted to check and see how things were at your end. What are you doing?"

"I'm eating pizza – extra cheese and pepperoni with black olives and onions. For dessert I'm having beef jerky. What about you?"

Shelly's stomach grumbled at the mention of pizza. Beef jerky she could do without, but she realized that she was hungry. “We had peanuts on the plane,” she said. “We’re on our way to Miss Phoenix now. When I figure out where we are going to stay tonight, I’ll give you a call.”

“Okay,” said Dakota. “Good luck.”

They hung up. Shelly was still mad at him but, oddly, she was glad he was there. She felt better after talking to him.

“Are you hungry?” she asked Sarra.

“Yes, very much,” Sarra nodded vigorously making the dark curls on her head bob.

“Excuse me!” Shelly had to yell and then tap the cabbie on his shoulder to get his attention.

“Hello, little chickadee,” he grinned at her. “What can I help you with?”

Great, thought Shelly, another person with a pet name mania. He would probably like her Gamma Brooks. They could sit around and call each other funny names.

“Is there a place where we could pull in for a hamburger or something? We’re kind of hungry.”

“Of course, little magpie. There are many places, but I do not allow anyone, even little birdlets like you, to eat in my cab,” he said. Shelly could not see his eyes hidden behind his dark glasses, but she saw him smile. He had big square teeth, but his mouth curled in at the corners in a friendly way. “But I could stop for a munchy-crunch my own self and so it will be!”

And he was as good as his word. They pulled

through a fast food restaurant and ordered. Then the cabbie drove them to a little park where they all got out of the cab and sat on a bench and ate their sandwiches.

"This is very nice," said Shelly. "Thank you."

"You are very welcome," the man took a huge bite of his hamburger and devoured almost the whole thing in that single bite. Shelly thought how impressed Dakota would have been.

"What is your name?" she asked.

"People call me Mr. Byrd. That's with a *y*, my friends," he said. "And that's on account of all the birds, with an *i,* with which I am acquainted."

"What does that mean?" asked Sarra.

"Here, I will show you," said Mr. Byrd. He put down the remains of his hamburger and then, after carefully wiping his mouth on a napkin, he pursed his lips together and created a trilling little whistle.

"That's cool," said Shelly.

"Very pretty," Sarra agreed smiling.

But Mr. Byrd held up his hand for silence and whistled again. He tilted his head to one side as though listening and, once more, trilled his peculiar whistle into the air.

And then, suddenly, to the delight of both Shelly and Sarra, the air around them was filled with about a dozen small, colorful birds.

CHAPTER FOURTEEN

TWILA PHOENIX

About the size of sparrows, the birds wore beautiful sky blue hoods with a peach blush over their tiny chests. They hopped around on the ground near Mr. Byrd's feet and the big man scattered some seeds for them, which he had in his pockets.

"What are they?" asked Sarra in delight.

"These are called Lazuli Buntings," said Mr. Byrd. "Lazuli, do you know, is the beautiful blue stone of the Egyptian pharaohs. These little fellows have been touched by the ancient gods, I should think." Mr. Byrd pursed his lips and whistled again only softer this time. The birds seemed to answer him with soft chirpings of their own.

"And of course that little fellow over there, the speckled one wearing that snazzy little brown cap,

that's a chipping sparrow. I see him around."

"You know a lot about birds," said Shelly.

"Of course I do, little limpkin," said Mr. Byrd grinning at her. "When I'm not driving a cab I'm a fully qualified ornithologist."

"What's an ornithologist?" asked Sarra.

"It's a scientist who studies birds," said Mr. Byrd.

"Shelly wants to be a scientist too," Sarra informed him.

"Of course she does," said Mr. Byrd. "Nothing better to be than a scientist, unless of course it's a poet or artist or explorer or cook or cabdriver. What kind of scientist?"

"A paleontologist," said Shelly.

"Excellent," said Mr. Byrd. "You'll be visiting La Brea then I presume."

"Yes, we will," said Shelly excitedly. "Have you been there? What's it like?"

"I've been there and it's like nothing you've ever seen before," said Mr. Byrd finishing his burger and slurping down about a half gallon of pop. "But for now I'd better get you to your destination of 2314 Orange Terrace. And here is my card. When you are ready to go to La Brea and if you need a ride, just give me a jingle."

Mr. Byrd flapped his large hand and the little birds fluttered into the sky. Shelly and Sarra picked up all the paper from their meal and put it in an old garbage can leaning near the curb. They all got back inside the cab and Mr. Byrd, with another loud song bubbling out of his throat, put the car in motion.

It took them about another 20 minutes to reach the address that Shelly had given Mr. Byrd. Orange Terrace proved to be an older neighborhood up a winding hill and on a dead end. Number 2314 was a pink stucco house with a small sandy looking yard at the end of the street.

"Here we are then," said Mr. Byrd. "It was very nice to meet you two and I hope you enjoy your visit in Los Angeles. Please give me a jingle if you need a ride."

"Thanks," said Shelly. "We will."

The girls got out of the cab and watched as Mr. Byrd did a three-point turn in the middle of the street and drove away with a happy toot of his horn.

"Well," said Shelly. "Here we are. I hope somebody is home."

Sarra and Shelly walked up the tiny, cement walkway to the shaded porch of the house. Everything was very quiet. Shades were drawn over the front windows. Everything looked peaceful and deserted. It was too early in the evening for lights to appear inside the houses so they couldn't tell if anyone was home or not. Shelly took a deep breath and pushed the doorbell.

Somewhere in the depths of the little pink house thcy could hcar thc tiny jinglc of thc bell.

Nothing happened.

"Maybe you should try again," suggested Sarra. So Shelly pushed the button and, once again they could hear the muffled chime.

Still nothing.

"I guess no one is home," said Shelly suddenly feeling very discouraged.

"Well then, you guessed wrong, young lady," snapped a voice from the shadows next to the porch.

Startled, both Shelly and Sarra turned around to see an elderly woman wearing a large, floppy hat and oversized gardening gloves standing at the foot of the porch steps.

"I am not interested in buying any cookies or wrapping paper or magazine subscriptions. Thank you very much. Now go away." And the woman turned to leave.

"Please wait," said Shelly. "We aren't selling anything."

Reluctantly the woman turned back. Under the large brim of her hat Shelly could see a small face wrinkled and brown as an old tree trunk and two sharp black eyes that regarded the girls with piercing attention.

"I'm not answering any survey questions either," said the woman.

"Are you Twila Phoenix?" asked Shelly.

The snappy black eyes narrowed and the woman took a few steps closer staring intently at the girls.

“Why do you look familiar?” she jabbed a pair of garden trimmers at Sarra. “Do I know you?”

“Are you Twila Phoenix?” asked Sarra in her soft voice a bit terrified by this garden tool wielding old woman.

“I am. Who are you?”

“My name is Sarra Fenniche. We’re looking for my brother, Amine.”

The woman let out a sigh and a quick smile played around the corner of her mouth.

“Of course you are,” she said. “You’d better come inside.”

She stomped up the porch steps and pushed past Shelly. Opening the door she gestured them to follow her.

“Mind the alligator,” she said as she stepped into the dimness of her house.

CHAPTER FIFTEEN

THE WONDER ROOM

Shelly felt her legs start to noodle under her when she saw the menacing and very big shape of the alligator stretched full length in the hallway. Its head reared in the air and its mouth was open in a huge yawn revealing rows of dagger sharp teeth.

"Cornelious Rathmorgan the Second," said Miss Phoenix with a wave of her hand introducing the reptile.

Miss Phoenix stepped close to Shelly and Sarra. Her black eyes peered sharply from under the floppy brim of her hat. "He's the second because he ate the *first* Cornelious Rathmorgan," she whispered fiercely. "For breakfast!"

Sarra clutched Shelly's arm in fear and Shelly thought that maybe her heart had stopped beating, but then she saw Miss Phoenix take off her floppy garden hat and plunk it on the head of the alligator. And was that wheezing sound Miss Phoenix laughing?

"Sarra," Shelly managed to sort of gasp as she realized what was going on. "It isn't alive!"

And now they could both see that it wasn't. Not only had it not moved, now with Miss Phoenix's floppy hat on its head, it looked more silly than dangerous.

"It is like taxidermy," said Sarra with a relieved smile. "You know, like when a hunter has an animal stuffed as a trophy. My Grandfather had an animal in his shop like that once."

"Nice to have made your acquaintance, Mr. Rrrrrathmorgan," said Shelly rolling her *r's*. She patted the alligator on the tip of its ferocious looking snout. "But I much prefer bones to stuffy old alligators, thank you very much."

"This way, girls," came the voice of Miss Phoenix.

Sarra and Shelly edged past Cornelious Rathmorgan the Second who may have eaten Cornelious Rathmorgan the First for breakfast, and followed the voice of Miss Phoenix. They found her in a small room just off the hallway.

The red-gold sunlight of late afternoon spilled into the room through several windows. Dust motes swirled calmly in the air and Miss Phoenix stood in the center of one of the most amazing rooms Shelly had ever seen before.

“Welcome to my Wonder Room,” said Miss Phoenix. She looked like a wizard in overalls as she stood in the middle of the room. Her white hair, free from her hat, stuck out in wild curls all over her head and the sunlight made a nimbus around it.

“Jumping alligator skins,” Shelly breathed in disbelief. Her eyes went wide as she tried to take in everything at once.

The room was lined with an array of shelves that contained a cluttered collection of objects. Shelly could see odd and wonderful things. There seemed to be everything from antiquities, like old clocks and delicate vases, to stones and artifacts, like a giant spearhead. An iron bell the size of a large pumpkin rested on a shelf next to a variety of sea horses and flying fish frozen in mid-leap. Cases of ancient coins and medallions caught the sunlight under one window. Spears and swords and what looked like a small round boat made from bark were suspended from the ceiling.

“Is this a giant snail shell?” asked Sarra pointing to a huge, beautiful spiraled shell propped against the spine of an old, brown book.

“It’s a nautilus shell,” said Miss Phoenix nodding her head. “It is resting against a book about the travels of the explorer Ian Garden. He claimed to have found in the Arctic, an entrance into the hollow center of the world.”

“The world isn’t hollow,” said Shelly.

Miss Phoenix shrugged. “Of course, you know

best," she said. "And that," she pointed to a long, pale bone of spiral grooves that diminished to a delicate point and was displayed over the window, "is the horn of a unicorn."

"Unicorns don't exist either," said Shelly impatiently.

"Of course not," agreed Miss Phoenix with a frown. "I myself am 87 years old and I never saw one."

But Shelly was only momentarily distracted from her own discoveries. Moving deeper into the room she began to see more and more marvels. Behind a huge fan of pink coral Shelly spied the delicate carvings of a tiny village complete with tiny people walking with small woven baskets on their heads and miniature dogs running at their heels.

"All carved from pumpkin seeds," said Miss Phoenix.

A dusty photograph proved to be a picture of two men standing beside a huge fish head the size of a small truck. A hand lettered caption read: "Loch Ness Monster head found by Neil and Jeremy Nichols."

"Loch Ness monster," Shelly snorted.

"A Miss-Know-It-All, I see," murmured Miss Phoenix.

"I'm a scientist," said Shelly. "I don't believe in fairy tales.

"Quite right too," said Miss Phoenix. "Imagination. Very dangerous."

Shelly was about to respond but she was interrupted.

"Shelly, look at this!" said Sarra motioning to her friend. "Look what's over here!"

Shelly hurried over to see what her friend had found. Beside a glass case, holding a carefully labeled collection of minerals, was a gray slab of stone. Sarra pointed to it.

"Look, Shelly," she said. "A Fish."

"A fossilized fish," said Shelly excitedly.

"*Coelacanthus*," said Miss Phoenix. "Thought extinct until one was caught off the coast of Madagascar in 1938. Can you imagine? It was like a fairy tale come to life."

Shelly opened her mouth to say something, but Miss Phoenix didn't seem to notice. "And that of course," she pointed to a large bone propped in the corner so deep in shadow Shelly had missed it before, "is the leg bone of a *diatryma*."

"Oh my goodness," said Shelly in amazement. "I've read about *diatryma*."

"Of course you have," said Miss Phoenix. "All good scientists read. What did you learn?"

"*Diatryma* was a terrifying, giant flightless bird," said Shelly sounding like a small professor giving a lecture. "It grew to be 7 to 9 feet tall. It had large muscled legs with 3 toes on each foot. It lived after the dinosaurs were all gone and some scientists think that it hunted mammals."

"And some scientists think it used its long sharp beak to cut through the fibers of tough plants," said Miss Phoenix. "Scientists. They can never agree on anything." She shook her head and sighed. "Curious bunch of people though, I'll say that for them. They are always poking things to see what will happen. That's what Cornelious Rathmorgan was doing when he got eaten for breakfast. Poking."

Suddenly Shelly spotted what looked like a pile of feathers on the floor next to the *Diatryma* bone. She crouched down next to it for a closer look. "What's this?" she asked.

"Oh, don't touch that!" warned Miss Phoenix.

But it was too late. Even as the warning came, Shelly, like other scientists before her, was already probing the unknown by poking the small mound of feathers with her finger.

There was a terrible squawk and Shelly jumped back as the feathers moved and something bit her finger!

CHAPTER SIXTEEN

GLADIATOR

"Ouch!" Shelly cried shaking her hand. There was a small sharp pain in her finger and it was bleeding.

"Oh dear," said Miss Phoenix rushing over. "Here. I'm pretty sure you will live. Wrap your finger in this and let's get that taken care of." She handed Shelly a flowered handkerchief.

"Gladiator, you are very bad," Miss Phoenix scolded the pile of feathers that glared up at them out of red-rimmed angry eyes. "It isn't manners at all to go around biting small scientists on their tender fingers. You should be ashamed of yourself."

But Gladiator gave a cranky squawk and absolutely refused to look ashamed. Instead he rose to his feet and revealed himself to be a rather large and irritable looking rooster with a beautiful fall of green

and gold tail feathers.

"What is it?" asked Sarra backing away towards the door.

"It's Gladiator," said Miss Phoenix with one arm around Shelly. "Are you okay, dear?"

Shelly nodded. "Yes. He didn't hurt me very badly. He surprised me though. I wasn't expecting to be attacked by a pile of old feathers."

"I know. I should have warned you. Gladiator likes to come in here because it is warm. He falls asleep

in the sun. Lately, he's been terribly cranky. I think he's sick. See how he is losing feathers?"

The girls looked down at Gladiator who, now that he was standing, shook out his elegant feathers and preened—just a little. His tail feathers were a brilliant green and reddish gold. His proud crimson comb stood up straight on his head. The rest of his feathers were a sleek black, but Shelly could see where one or two small feathers remained on the floor where Gladiator had been sleeping.

Suddenly Gladiator stood on tiptoe, worked his wings up and down, stretched his long neck so that the feathers there fanned out and let loose with a loud ringing crow.

"Yikes!" Sarra clasped her hands over her ears and quickly got out of the way as Gladiator, ruffling his feathers back in place, stalked out of the room.

"Well," said Shelly examining the damage to her finger. "He sure is a fighter. I can see why he's named Gladiator."

"He's a fighting rooster, that's true," said Miss Phoenix. "I rescued him one day after he had been in a terrible fight. He crawled into my back garden. When he got better though he turned out to have a very sweet temperament. He much prefers looking handsome to fighting in the dirt and dust. But recently he has gotten very touchy. So come along you two, time for something to eat and a bandage."

Miss Phoenix bustled the girls out of the room,

but just as they were leaving Sarra caught sight of something sitting far back on a shelf. It was something that looked like the fossil skull she had drawn for PaleoJoe!

"Miss Phoenix," said Sarra as they followed the woman into her tiny kitchen. "Do you know my brother Amine?"

"Yes, of course I do," said Miss Phoenix. "And I will tell you all about it, but first let's get things settled here."

Outside the day was gathering the shadows of evening. Miss Phoenix turned on lights, helped Shelly clean, disinfect her wounded finger and bandage it. Then she set about slicing some cheese and apples, banging cupboards open and rattling dishes, and humming as she worked. In a small microwave oven she popped a bag of popcorn and the delicious salty smell filled the house.

Gladiator stalked in and Miss Phoenix put down a plate of grains for him. Keeping one red-rimmed eye fiercely on the intruders in his kitchen, the rooster poked and plucked at the grain, sometimes flinging bits and pieces to the far corners of the kitchen.

"Now then," said Miss Phoenix as she and Sarra and Shelly settled around the kitchen table munching on the delicious snack, "where are you two planning on spending the night?"

Shelly and Sarra looked at each other in dismay. They had completely forgotten about finding a hotel. It

was getting late, and suddenly Shelly realized she was feeling very tired indeed. It had been a longer day than usual.

"Thought so," said Miss Phoenix nodding and pursing her lips together. "Two adventurers on their own. Well, never mind. Nothing like a good adventure or two to liven things up. I have a spare room and you will stay with me."

"Thank you," said Shelly. "We really came to see you to find out about Sarra's brother, Amine."

Miss Phoenix nodded and munched on a slice of apple. "I knew that the minute I saw Sarra. She has her Granddad's eyes and so does her brother."

"How did you know my Grandfather?" asked Sarra.

"Well, that was an adventure all my own, young lady," said Miss Phoenix her face crinkling in a smile. "We started out to be very good friends, your Granddad and me. He was a rowdy young fellow who loved adventures and getting into trouble."

For some reason Shelly suddenly thought about Dakota. Dakota liked adventure and he certainly seemed to be in trouble a lot. Constantly, in fact.

"Do you know that Grandfather has passed away?" asked Sarra in a small, sad voice.

"Yes, dear," said Miss Phoenix quietly. "Your brother told me that Cadi was very sick and that he would not be getting better.

"Your Granddad Cadi was quite a fellow though,

Sarra. He came out to work the old Salt Creek oil fields back in days longer ago then I care to count," said Miss Phoenix. "Probably can't count them really because they were so long ago. My own daddy was the fellow who hired the boys to come and work in those fields, but I was there all the time. The fields were rich in treasures and even way back then I was collecting for my Wonder Room you know."

"What kind of treasures?" asked Shelly awkwardly scooping a handful of buttery salty popcorn with her left hand to keep salt from getting into her wounded finger.

"The fossils of course," said Miss Phoenix. "The old Salt Creek oil fields were 7 miles west of Los Angeles but today, they are in the very middle of the downtown. Times can sure change on a person."

"La Brea Tar Pits!" said Shelly and Sarra together.

"Right! And that's how I knew your Granddad, Sarra. The boys working the fields were always finding bones and fossils. Whenever your Granddad found something he thought was special, he gave it to me. At least for awhile he did. Then we had a huge, old, crack down fight and he went away and I never saw him again."

"What did you fight about?" asked Shelly and then realized it was probably none of her business and the question had been rude. But Miss Phoenix didn't seem to notice.

"Can't remember now. He was such a knucklehead. I liked him though. I'm sorry we fought because then he went back home to Morocco. Never said good-bye. And I never saw him again." Miss Phoenix sighed.

"We got a postcard from my brother saying he was staying here with you and that he was on a mission from my Grandfather," said Sarra.

"Amine did stay with me for about a week. But that was, let me see...2 years ago. Yes. 2 years ago. I don't see him very often, and he won't tell me where he is staying, but he does check in on me now and then. He is still trying to complete his mission."

"What is his mission?" asked Shelly.

But before Miss Phoenix could answer, Shelly's phone rang.

Twice.

Then it was silent.

"Uh-oh," said Shelly. "The Disaster Signal."

CHAPTER SEVENTEEN

THE GAME IS UP

Dakota was watching his favorite Detective T.V. show when the phone rang. And because the hero, a street tough, wisecracking detective by the name of Dexter North, was closing in on the criminals, and because Dakota wanted to see if his own guess about who was guilty was going to be correct, he allowed his mother to answer the phone. And because the commercial break was still ten minutes away, Dakota was completely absorbed in whether the criminal's game was up or not and did not notice much of anything else. Eyes riveted to the T.V. screen, Dakota was only sort of aware when his mom came into the living room and sat down on the sofa to watch him with a frown on her face.

When the commercial finally did arrive, aggravatingly, Dakota was still in the dark as to who the criminal was. He still did not notice the concerned look of concentration on the face of his mother and by then he had forgotten that the phone had rung at all.

It wasn't until the doorbell rang and his mom ushered in PaleoJoe, Gamma Brooks, and Mrs. Fenniche and turned off the T.V. that Dakota realized his own game was up.

"Dakota," his mother said fixing him with that Mom-look that plainly communicates the need for complete honesty in order to avoid death, "where are Shelly and Sarra?"

"They're in Los Angeles," said Dakota feeling his stomach sink to somewhere below his heels.

Gamma Brooks gasped and Mrs. Fenniche put her hand on her heart as though she were going to faint. PaleoJoe looked like he was going to explode his face was so red.

"But they're okay," said Dakota quickly. He shifted from one foot to the other, feeling very much like he wanted to run away. His palms were sweaty and he felt a little weak in his knees. He was in big trouble and he knew it.

"Thank goodness for that," said Gamma Brooks and now she began to look a little angry too as she glared at Dakota over the tops of her glasses.

Desperately, Dakota looked at Sarra's mom. She was a tall, pretty woman with black curly hair like her daughter. Her dark eyes had the same worried look in them that Dakota had seen in the eyes of his own mother, but she didn't look so much angry as she looked concerned. Dakota appealed to her.

"Mrs. Fenniche," he said. "Sarra went to look for Amine. She knows where to find him. She didn't have time to tell you because the police were going to come and arrest her."

"What?!" Mrs. Fenniche turned very pale. Dakota realized that he hadn't put that very well.

"Dakota, what are you talking about?" said PaleoJoe. "Sit down here and stop jittering around like a jack rabbit. Tell us what happened."

So Dakota told them the whole story. When he finished there was a brief moment of silence as the adults looked at each other.

At last PaleoJoe let out a gusty sigh and stroked his beard in agitation. "You overheard me talking to Detective Franks about a possible smuggling case out in Seattle," he said. "It had nothing to do with Sarra and her story."

"We didn't know that," said Dakota. "Sarra was scared and we needed to act fast. I gave them my essay plane tickets. We had the plan all worked out."

Then the adults all started talking at once. In

the blur of voices Dakota sat feeling miserable. He had to think of some way to warn Shelly they had been discovered. She would not have much time to find Amine if she and Sarra were made to come home.

"There really is only one thing to do," said PaleoJoe when the rush of discussion died down. "I'll get on a plane tonight and go after them. Dakota, do you know where they are exactly?"

"Well, not exactly. At least not yet," he added seeing fresh anger building in Gamma Brooks. "Shelly will call when she and Sarra check into a hotel. That should be any time now."

"In any case," said PaleoJoe, "we know they plan to visit La Brea Tar Pits. I should be able to find them there."

"That sounds like a good plan to me," said Gamma Brooks.

"Me too," said Mrs. Fenniche.

"Not me," said Dakota earning himself more glares from the adults. "What I mean is, I'm part of this adventure too and I think I should go along with PaleoJoe to help him."

He saw PaleoJoe begin to shake his head and he already knew his mom was thinking no, so borrowing a technique sometimes employed by Shelly Brooks, Dakota launched Maximum Force Questioning.

"Howwillyouknowwhattheirplanisif youdon'ttakemealongwithyouandhow willyoufindthemifyoudon'tknowwhere tolookforthemanddon'tyouthinkitwou ldbeagoodthingformetocomealongtoo?"

It was like fighting with pepper. PaleoJoe blinked rapidly several times and cleared his throat. "It's okay with me if Dakota wants to come," he said.

And Dakota's mom just nodded her head.

Without appearing too joyful over getting his way, Dakota stood up. "I'll just go pack my bag."

As he left the room he heard the murmur of adult voices begin again. Quickly he ducked into the kitchen and dialed Shelly's cell phone number. He let the phone ring two times and then he hung up.

CHAPTER EIGHTEEN

DIRE WOLVES and DEXTER NORTH

PaleoJoe and Dakota were in the air by 8:00 that evening. Sitting next to PaleoJoe on the airplane Dakota was uncomfortably reminded of his anxiety dream. He still had not learned to skydive and so he hoped that this plane would remain in the air and that no one would push him out if it while it was flying.

It was dark and the stars were sharp pinpoints of light in the sky. Beside him PaleoJoe was reading a tattered old book. Dakota watched him turn the yellowed pages and then snuck a peek at the title. *Dinosaurs of the World.*

Definitely not as exciting as a Dexter North

adventure, thought Dakota to himself.

Dakota dug in his backpack, found his pair of dark sunglasses and put them on. He turned up the collar of his jacket, slouched in his seat and cautiously stuck his head out into the aisle. He couldn't really see anything in the dimness of the plane interior while he was wearing his sunglasses because the lights had been turned down to allow the passengers to sleep if they wanted.

Dakota eased back in his seat. In the chair pocket in front of him was a travel magazine. Using two fingers Dakota eased the magazine out of its pocket and casually tossed it on the aisle floor. As he leaned out of his chair to retrieve it he looked up and down the aisle of seated passengers seeing mostly ankles and feet.

As he leaned back into his seat he suddenly became aware that PaleoJoe was watching him. He pretended a giant yawn and the left lens of his sunglasses popped out and fell in his lap.

"What are you doing?" asked PaleoJoe.

Dakota looked at him. He looked like a strange alien with one dark lens in and just his green, mischievous eye peering out the other, lens free circle.

"I'm pretending to be Dexter North and I'm sussing out the plane," he said. He popped his lens back in place and discovered he had put it in upside down. It didn't quite fit the frame.

"Sussing?" PaleoJoe raised an eyebrow.

"Yeah, you know, checking things out for a crime. Dexter North does it all the time. That's how he finds the criminals. He susses."

"I see," PaleoJoe's face twitched as he smothered a laugh. Dakota didn't seem to notice as he struggled with his sunglasses lens.

"PaleoJoe," said Dakota. "Can I ask you something?"

"Of course," said PaleoJoe. He carefully closed his book and stowed it away in his pack. He knew that Dakota had something on his mind and he had been waiting for him to begin talking about it.

Dakota put his sunglasses back on and took a deep breath. Then he told PaleoJoe all about winning the essay contest and about his argument with Shelly. He finished by telling PaleoJoe how Shelly had accused him of cheating.

"I didn't cheat," said Dakota. "I borrowed that book from you and I did some research in the library and I just wrote that essay. It was hard. It had to be 300 words or less and it was hard." Dakota wrinkled his face in concentration as he tried to express what he was feeling. "You know, PaleoJoe, I don't get very good grades in school sometimes, but when I wrote that essay I wasn't thinking about that."

"What were you thinking about?" asked PaleoJoe.

"I was thinking about how great Dire Wolves were," said Dakota. "I just really wanted people to know that. I just wanted to tell the story the best way I could."

"I'd like to read your essay sometime," said PaleoJoe.

"Well, that's what I wanted to ask you," said Dakota. He reached into his backpack and pulled out a sheaf of papers neatly stapled together. "Here's a copy of my essay. Would you read it and tell me why you think I won and Shelly didn't? Shelly is way smarter than me. I know that. She should have won."

"Read it to me," said PaleoJoe and settled back in his seat to listen.

Dakota had to take off his sunglasses so he could see and then he began to read.

CHAPTER NINETEEN

THE FATE OF FANG AND THE MYSTERY OF PETROLEUM

The howl of wolves echoed in the cold air. The Dire Wolves were on the hunt. Leading this pack was a Dire Wolf called Fang. He was a big wolf, over five feet long, and he weighed more than 110 pounds. Today, Fang's pack had been on the trail of a group of horses. One of the horses was sick and the wolves knew that soon they would be able to isolate it from the herd.

The Ice Age Dire Wolves were the largest wolves to ever live. They were related to the Gray Wolf, but they were much larger than wolves today. They had large and powerful teeth that they used to crush the

bones of their prey.

Many Dire Wolf bones have been found in the La Brea Tar Pits in Los Angeles, California. Some of the bones show healed injuries that could have been the result of being kicked or stepped on during the pursuit of larger animals of prey.

Running across the open ground, the pack closed in on the horses. One horse, unable to keep up with the rest, fell behind. With Fang in the lead, the wolves attacked.

Fang lived a long time for a Dire Wolf. When he was old he died along the banks of a river. In 1854 some of his bones were found by Francis Lick on the banks of the Ohio River near Evansville, Indiana. These were the first Dire Wolf bones discovered.

Fang was named* Canis dirus *and became a legendary animal of the Pleistocene age.

Dakota stopped reading and PaleoJoe remained silent. Dakota felt a knot begin to form in the pit of his stomach. What was wrong?

Finally PaleoJoe spoke.

"Dakota," he said. "You won that essay contest because you didn't write just a report about Dire Wolves. You made them come to life. You told a story. When you read your essay I feel like I am really there with Fang and his pack."

Dakota smiled and felt very happy. He leaned back in his seat and took off his sunglasses. "Thanks,

PaleoJoe," he said.

"And Shelly will understand eventually," PaleoJoe added. "But you can understand how disappointed she must feel."

Dakota nodded. "So PaleoJoe," he said deciding to change the subject. "I was just wondering about these tar pits. Are they like quicksand? Do they just sort of suck their victims down into a black sticky goo and suffocate them? Where does the tar come from? What's the story?"

PaleoJoe leaned back in his chair. "It is a story," he said. "Do you want to hear it?"

"Okay," said Dakota. "But when that lady with the cart comes by again I want a pop, please. I'm very thirsty."

PaleoJoe grinned. "Right. The asphalt of La Brea Tar Pits comes from petroleum. Now, here's a question, Mr. Detective, what do you know about petroleum?"

"It's like gasoline," said Dakota. "It comes out of the pumps at the gas station."

"Really?" asked PaleoJoe lifting one eyebrow in that move that Dakota greatly envied.

"Well," said Dakota trying to imitate the raised eyebrow, but only managing to wiggle both of them in a goofy sort of way. "There are these pipes see, and they go from the gas station pumps down into the center of the earth where there are these pools of tar. The pipes suck the tar up into the pumps and..." Dakota stopped when he saw the look PaleoJoe was giving him. "Ah, actually I have no idea," he admitted.

The cart lady came by just then and PaleoJoe got them both sodas.

"Listen and learn, boy," he said popping the tab on his can of pop.

Dakota did the same resisting the impulse to shake it first and took a quick gulp of his soda. "I'm listening, oh great Paleontologist," he said hiccupping a bit from the sudden onslaught of bubbles in his stomach.

"You have to think of the creation of petroleum like a recipe," said PaleoJoe. "The first ingredients are living plants and animals. Living organisms contain carbon."

"Is that the same element that's found in pencil lead?" asked Dakota surprising PaleoJoe and proving that, at times, he could be intelligent.

"That's right," said PaleoJoe. "And it's carbon combined with oxygen that is making the fizz in your pop."

"Cool!" said Dakota and then he burped. "It wasn't me! It was the carbon!" he tried to defend himself without laughing. After all, in certain circles, Dakota was well known for his burping artistry.

"And it's the carbon that turns into oil," said PaleoJoe choosing to ignore Dakota's bad manners.

"Just a minute," said Dakota. He flipped open his memo book and wrote the heading: A Recipe for Oil. "Okay. Continue."

"Like Fang, organisms die," said PaleoJoe

watching Dakota take careful notes as he spoke. "Normally when plants or animals die the carbon they contain combines with oxygen to produce carbon dioxide gas. This is the process of decomposition.

"But sometimes oxygen is cut off if the dead plant or animal is covered by mud. In a case like that the carbon in the organism is trapped and then it might turn into oil."

"How exactly?" asked Dakota.

"Two more ingredients are added," said PaleoJoe impressed by Dakota's note taking. "Time and Temperature. At La Brea the organisms that provided most of the carbon for the oil were tiny microscopic plants and animals called plankton."

"We learned about those in science class," said Dakota eagerly. "They live in the water."

"That's right," said PaleoJoe. "Where La Brea is today was once covered by the Pacific Ocean which was the home to millions of plankton. As the plankton died they drifted to bottom of the ocean where, if other animals did not eat them, they became covered with layers of sediment. Over time as much as five miles of sediment buried them. The pressure of this weight squeezed out the water and pressed the particles of sand and mud tightly together trapping layers of dead plankton.

"This created a type of rock known as sedimentary rock."

"I've heard of that too," said Dakota and paused

in his note taking to drink his pop.

"Temperatures increased as the rock got pressed deeper and deeper into the ground," continued PaleoJoe. "When rock is pressed 8,000 feet into the earth it is exposed to temperatures of about 175 degrees to 275 degrees Fahrenheit. That's hot enough to begin changing plankton carbon into oil.

"But it didn't happen overnight," said PaleoJoe looking out of the plane window into the darkness of the sky. "The conversion takes 5 to 50 million years."

"Wow," said Dakota yawning. "That's a long time."

"And so," said PaleoJoe, "after the ocean receded the great pressure within the earth pushed that oil upwards, and about 40,000 years ago it began to leak out through the loose sand and gravel at La Brea."

"And the death traps were born," finished Dakota.

CHAPTER TWENTY

SWING TIME

While PaleoJoe and Dakota were flying through the night in relative comfort discussing Dire Wolves and petroleum, Shelly and Sarra were getting ready to spend the night with Miss Phoenix. Shelly had waited for Dakota to call her back, but so far he had not. When she tried to call him she got a busy signal.

Well, she reasoned, he would call her when he could and then she would find out what the panic was, but for now she was really too tired to be worried about much.

Both girls were enormously sleepy as Miss Phoenix showed them to her guest room, which turned out to be her back porch. The porch was screened in and a fragrant night breeze gently drifted through carrying with it the buzz and whir of night insects. Sevcral potted palm trees gave the room a very tropical feeling. It was a wonderful place and Shelly could only see one thing wrong with it—there wasn't a bed. Two wicker rocking chairs did not look promising as a place to sleep.

"No doubt you are wondering if I am going to make you sleep on the floor," chuckled Miss Phoenix. "And the answer is no. Only Gladiator sleeps on the floor. It is comfortable for a rooster but not for young scientists and the granddaughter of my old friend."

"Are we going to sleep in those chairs then?" asked Sarra puzzled.

"Well you can if you want to, of course," said Miss Phoenix. "But I would suggest you try my beds instead. But I have to warn you. They are the most comfortable beds you will ever sleep in. In fact you may never want to get out of them once you get into them. Of course," she added mysteriously, "getting into them is sometimes a bit of a challenge."

As she talked she opened an enormous trunk that was pushed against one wall.

"This is my elephant's trunk," she said chuckling. "I call it that because it's big enough to probably hold an elephant, but also because it has elephants carved on it."

She wrestled out a couple of bundles of what looked like nets.

"Of course I am 87 years old," she snapped at the watching girls, " and could use a little help here!"

Shelly and Sarra sprang into action. It turned out that the bundles of nets were hammocks. Miss Phoenix showed the girls where there were hooks in the walls and soon two hammocks were strung and ready for occupancy. Miss Phoenix rummaged in the elephant's trunk for the final items of two lightweight blankets and two pillows fringed with golden tassels.

"Now then," she said. "I'm going to bed. You two best do the same. Tomorrow we will go to the tar pits and we will look for Amine. Be careful getting into bed."

She left laughing to herself. Sarra and Shelly looked a little nervously at their gently swaying beds.

"How hard can it be?" asked Shelly.

She went over to one of the beds. Standing on tiptoe she just managed to settle her backside onto the edge of the hammock, which promptly flipped over depositing her on the floor.

"*Oof*!" said Shelly. Her breath was knocked out of her and as she lay on the hard floor she thought that maybe this is what it might feel like to be bowled over by an actual elephant. "Well, that didn't work out very well."

She got up and tried again. This time she tried getting in by leaning forward onto the swaying hammock. The netting caught her, scooped her off her feet, and helplessly her face was pressed down against the ropes on the hammock, her arms and legs flailed uselessly in the air. She was like a great, netted fish.

Sarra began to laugh.

"It's not funny!" said Shelly irritated. Only, because her face was smashed into the netting of the hammock, it came out like this: "Ish not funnish."

"Yes it is!" gasped Sarra.

"Help pish," said Shelly.

Sarra, laughing so hard now she could barely stand, pulled Shelly's legs until the hammock off balanced again and flung both of them onto the floor.

Now Shelly was laughing, too. "This is never going to work."

For the next several minutes Sarra and Shelly tried various strategies for getting into the hammock, each resulting in spectacular entrapment or swift ejection onto the ground. Finally, with tears streaming down their faces, they lay in a heap on the floor completely dissolved in hysterical laughter.

"I guess we'll have to sleep on the floor after all," said Sarra gulping down hiccups of laughter.

"Not if I can help it," said Shelly with determination. "I'm not going to be beaten by a bunch of knotted string!"

She marched across the room and got one of the wicker rocker chairs. The chair was very

big with a large fanned back. Shelly managed to half carry and half drag it over to the side of her hammock. Then, carefully standing on the chair, which rocked unsteadily beneath her, she strategized her movement, and fell backward into the very middle of the hammock.

"Whoohoo!" she yelled. "Success!" The hammock swayed, but she was safely in the center of it and, she realized, Miss Phoenix had been absolutely right. It was extremely comfortable.

She heard Sarra struggle with the other chair and then with another *yippee!* her friend was also wrapped snugly in bed.

"Good night, Sarra," said Shelly sleepily.

"Good night, Shelly," yawned Sarra.

And all was quiet. For a moment. Shelly began to drift off to sleep when suddenly, the sharp trilling of a phone broke the gentle quietness of the night.

"It's your cell phone!" said Sarra.

"I know it is," said Shelly. "It's in my backpack which is in the corner of the room. There isn't any thing I can do about it. I'm not getting out of this hammock again. I might not ever be able to get back into it." She began to count the rings. One, two, three, four, five, six....

The ringing went on and then it stopped, but by that time Shelly was snoring very gently and was sound asleep.

CHAPTER TWENTY-ONE

LA BREA

In the morning the first thing Shelly did was to dig out her cell phone. Flipping it open she discovered a low battery and 5 missed calls from Gamma Brooks that gave her serious knots in her stomach. She would, she knew, have to deal with that, but first she wanted to talk to Dakota. When she got through to him, she was very surprised to discover that he and PaleoJoe were in Los Angeles, too.

"Are we in serious trouble?" Shelly demanded, feeling her nerves jumping like a high voltage charge. "Because Sarra is seriously concerned here and I think she might faint or something. I mean, right now, I'm looking right at her and I think she is turning purple or something with panic and is going to faint right here right in front of me!"

From her gently swaying hammock, Sarra blinked sleepily at Shelly without the smallest trace of panic. Shelly realized it wasn't Sarra at all who was at the extreme end of worry—it was herself. She turned her back on Sarra and began to bite at her thumbnail. "Dakota," she said, "How deep are we in trouble?"

"On a scale of one to ten with ten being in pretty deep—I'd say we're at about a 25," said Dakota helpfully. "I think I may be grounded until I'm ready to retire. Did you find Sarra's brother yet?"

"No," said Shelly. "We're heading to La Brea Tar Pits this morning to look."

Shelly heard some muffled mumbles that sounded like someone had stuffed Dakota's phone in a sock. But then she realized that Dakota was just consulting PaleoJoe and had probably covered the phone with his hand while they talked things over. She waited patiently.

"PaleoJoe says we'll meet you there," said Dakota coming back on the line. "He said rendezvous by the wall of wolf skulls."

"That sounds a bit gruesome," said Shelly.

"I bet it's nothing to the look on his face right now," said Dakota. "Hey—"

Now Shelly heard something that sounded like someone getting thunked with a pillow and then Dakota was back.

"I gotta go, Shelly," he said. "PaleoJoe needs coffee or something really badly. He seems to have no sense of humor..."

And that was as far as he got when the phone went dead due to the fact that PaleoJoe had decided Dakota had chattered on enough, and that coffee was indeed of immediate concern.

Shelly's next phone call was to Gamma Brooks.

"I am glad you are safe, munchkin," said Gamma, but her voice was not soft and warm. "We will discuss this when you return with PaleoJoe. Sarra's mother is here with me and she is very concerned, too, you know."

"I know," said Shelly. "And I'm sorry we worried you, but Gamma it's important that we find Sarra's brother."

"And I know that, pipkin. So find him and then come home."

Sarra watched as Shelly disconnected with Gamma. The unhappy frown on Shelly's face told the whole story.

"I'm sorry to get you into trouble," said Sarra.

"It's okay," said Shelly. "It was my choice to help. I guess we're in trouble all right, but we still need to find your brother."

"And I am ready now to do that," said Sarra and she began to energetically flail her arms and legs in the air.

"Are you exercising?" asked Shelly.

"No," wailed Sarra, her arms and legs whipping up and down rocking the hammock into a vigorous

swing. "I can't get out of this thing! Help!"

Laughing, Shelly helped Sarra get out of the hammock by spilling her out onto the floor.

"Ow," said Sarra rubbing her backside. "That was certainly worse than fainting."

"I think I agree," said Shelly in sympathy. "But it's time to get moving."

Once more she flipped open her cell phone and made a call to Mr. Byrd.

"I will arrive in 10 minutes, little Oriole," he said.

And he was as good as his word. When he arrived Shelly took him to meet Miss Phoenix and Gladiator. She thought that maybe, with all his knowledge about birds, he could tell Miss Phoenix if Gladiator was sick.

Mr. Byrd frowned at the rooster and shook his head. "Not much wrong with this fellow, Chickadee," he told Shelly. "All he needs is a hen or two to boss around."

"Of course!" shouted Miss Phoenix. "I should have guessed that!" And without further discussion of the matter she donned her floppy garden hat grabbed a very big straw handbag and set off to find some hens for Gladiator.

"I'll try down at the Farmer's Market," she said as she banged out of the house. "Enjoy the tar pits. Come back tonight for dinner and stay with me again if you want to." She waved her hand as she hurried away down the street.

"Come along, little Pipers," said Mr. Byrd and ushered Shelly and Sarra into his taxi. "You have great adventures waiting!"

The morning traffic was very heavy. Shelly had never been on a road that had five lanes all going in the same direction and all filled with cars. It was very exciting, but it also felt very crowded.

"*My Wild Irish Rose*," sang Mr. Byrd in a loud deep voice as they moved along in the almost bumper-to-bumper traffic.

Outside the taxi the air was a blue hazy color, but the sun was bright and the chrome of the cars winked and flashed in the brightness of the day. It took Mr. Byrd almost a half hour to reach the famous Wilshire Boulevard on which La Brea Tar Pits were located. But finally they reached their destination and Mr. Byrd spun his taxi smoothly into the museum parking lot. Shelly and Sarra got out.

"Call me when you need to go home again, little pipers," said Mr. Byrd waving his large hand at them from his taxi window.

"Thank you," said Shelly waving back. "We will!"

"*Over hill over dale we have hit the dusty trail*," sang Mr. Byrd and revved his engine as he drove off.

"Now what?" said Sarra looking around.

They were right in the middle of the city. All around the perimeter of the parking lot rose tall,

silvered buildings. There were apartment buildings and office buildings and other buildings that Shelly could only guess about. All around them was the rush of a busy city. In the traffic of the boulevard horns honked in irritation at delays. The hum of traffic was a steady drone of sound. Pedestrians hurried along the sidewalks calling and shouting. Dogs barked. And in the far, far distance they could even hear the sounds of sirens.

"This sure is a busy place," said Shelly. "Come on, Sarra. The museum is over there."

Shelly pointed to a low curved building crowned by a stone panel of carvings and guarded by statues of fighting saber-toothed cats.

"Shelly, what's that black pool of water over there?" asked Sarra pointing to where the sidewalk curved away from the museum and traveled alongside a high wire fence that enclosed a large pond of black water.

"Let's take a closer look," said Shelly.

The girls left the sidewalk going right up to the fence and peering through. Up close the black water looked sluggish and gooey. Nearby, a mammoth family made from fiberglass was posed on the bank of the water. One of them had been caught in the black water, her trunk raised in alarm, and her graceful ivory colored tusks pierced the sky. Her baby, safe for the moment on shore, looked terrified at the danger his mother was in.

"That's not water," said Shelly. "It's bubbling."

“It must be tar,” said Sarra. “You can smell it.”

She was right. The air was heavy with a rotten egg smell. Shelly wrinkled her nose.

“Pewy,” she said. “Come on. Let’s look around.”

Shelly and Sarra walked among the small crowd of people milling in the park cntrance. Shelly looked sharply about to see if she could spot Dakota and PaleoJoe. She didn’t see them, but she did see a man, not too far away from them, suddenly duck out of sight behind a tree. Was it her imagination or had he done it deliberately as though to hide?

“Sarra,” said Shelly. “I think someone is spying on us.”

CHAPTER TWENTY-TWO

MISSING TOOTH

"I don't like the sound of that," said Sarra nervously. "Are you sure?"

"No," said Shelly. "It could have been my imagination. Come on. Let's go inside and see if we can find PaleoJoe. But keep your eyes open!"

Sarra and Shelly followed a small group of people into the Page museum. Once they stepped out of the bright morning sunlight into the interior of the museum they forgot, for the moment, about everything else.

Inside, the museum was a bit overwhelming. Shelly hardly knew what to look at first. Arranged in islands in the center of the large main floor and lining the walls were display cases of the reassembled bones of animals recovered from the tar pits.

"Wow!" said Shelly. "Look at all those skeletons! Come on! I want to take a good look at them."

In the center of the large open room was the huge skeleton of a mammoth. Its tusks curved gracefully from its massive jaw in a spectacular array of defense.

"I bet no one ever messed with him," said Shelly.

The murals painted on the walls caught Sarra's attention. They depicted beautifully painted scenes from the Pleistocene age in vivid detail.

"Look at this, Shelly," said Sarra pointing to a scene showing horse-like animals that looked almost like zebras trapped in the tar and being attacked by saber-toothed cats. "It must take a great amount of imagining to paint like that. Maybe someday I will be as good at painting."

"I bet you could do it," said Shelly. "You have drawing talent. PaleoJoe said so, remember?"

Sarra gazed a minute longer admiring the mural, but Shelly grew impatient. "Come on," she said. "What's over here?"

Shelly dragged Sarra from one display to the next. She was completely fascinated by the reconstructed animal skeletons. According to the information posted on each exhibit, Shelly spotted a Harlan sloth, a dwarf pronghorn, a Dire Wolf and a saber-toothed cat among many others. The skeletons were spectacular. The bones were a deep brown coffee color and so Shelly knew that they had been recovered from the tar.

"Look at all this information," said Shelly reading what amounted to a short book on the hunting habits of saber-toothed cats.

It was long thought that saber-toothed cats killed their prey by sinking their giant canines into the neck of their victims. By closely examining the well-preserved canines at La Brea, Paleontologists have rejected this theory. A study of bone injuries has led to a new picture of how Smilodon hunted. After a short run, the saber-toothed cat would leap onto its prey, grapple the prey over to expose the belly, and then kill it by gashing a large wound in the soft underside.

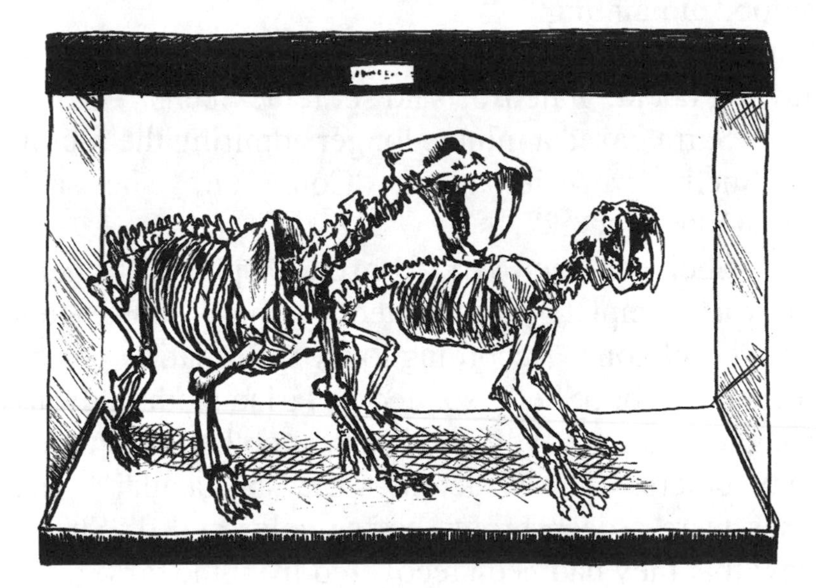

"I never knew that!" said Shelly.

It was while she was peering into the case of the saber-toothed cats that she caught a glimpse of a man in the reflection of the glass case. For a minute she thought it might be the same man she had seen hiding behind the tree. But when she turned around, she couldn't spot him.

"Come on Sarra," she grabbed Sarra's arm and pulled her friend over to another case. "Pretend to look at this for a minute," she said to Sarra under her breath.

Shelly positioned herself so she could see the reflections of people behind her in the case glass. Sure enough, the same man appeared again. His image was distorted in the glass and it was too dim to see many details, but Shelly could make out that he wore a blue baseball cap. Again, when she turned around he managed to disappear.

"We need to find that wall of skulls," said Shelly.

"Shelly, look!" Sarra pointed to the display case she had been looking at. "It's the Sabertooth skull!"

And it was. Or at least it was one very much like the sketch Sarra had shown PaleoJoe. It was resting in a case by itself. A small plaque next to the case explained about the exhibit. Shelly read it out loud.

Rare closed-mouthed Smilodon skull. This skull was excavated from the tar pits in the 1930's by

an unknown oil field worker. It is the only known Smilodon skull to be found with its mouth closed. This is special because it demonstrates exactly how the curved canines of Smilodon rested when the big cat closed its mouth.

A mystery: This skull is in possession of only one canine. What happened to the other one? Did the Smilodon lose it in battle? Was it lost in the excavation? Did it get separated from the skull during the process of coming to the museum?

"Look," said Shelly pointing to the skull. "You can see where the other canine should be. And it doesn't look like it broke off at all. It looks like it's just missing."

"Do you think the real tooth I have might be the missing one on this skull?" asked Sarra.

"Maybe," said Shelly. "PaleoJoe will know. We've got to find him."

"Only don't look now," said a deep and sinister sounding voice in Shelly's ear. "But someone is spying on you!"

CHAPTER TWENTY-THREE

AN INVITATION TO DIG

Shelly whirled around and stomped down hard on the foot of the person standing behind her.

It turned out to be Dakota. With a howl of pain he hopped up and down attracting the attention of all the people standing nearby.

"Ow! Ow! Ow!" he yelped. "Shelly Brooks, you broke my foot!"

"Good!" said Shelly facing him now with her hands on her hips. "That's what you get for scaring me half to death!"

"I was just joking!" said Dakota and tried tenderly to put his weight on his foot. "I didn't know you were going to attack me!"

The people around them began to lose interest and turned back to their own explorations of the museum. Shelly and Sarra allowed Dakota to lean on them and helped him hop over to a bench. Dakota massaged his foot and wiggled it around. It did not appear to be broken, but it still hurt.

"You're crackers," he said to Shelly.

"It's self defense," said Shelly.

"We think someone is following us," said Sarra interrupting the verbal battle that threatened to break out between Dakota and Shelly.

"Really?" Dakota looked interested. "Who?"

"We don't know," said Shelly. "We just made an interesting discovery when you barged in on us and we need to find PaleoJoe." "I didn't barge," said Dakota defensively. "I was looking for you. And I found you, too. That's because I am a great detective."

Sarra shook her head impatiently. How could these two fight all the time?

"Okay, Great Detective," said Shelly. "Where exactly is PaleoJoe?"

"PaleoJoe is over at the unbelievably cool Dire Wolf skull wall. He's talking to one of the museum paleontologists. What discovery did you make?"

"We'll tell you about it later," said Shelly. "Right now let's find PaleoJoe."

Dakota found he could walk on his foot just fine. He tried some pathetic limping just to make Shelly feel bad, but it didn't seem to be working and was only slowing them down, so he gave it up and guided Shelly and Sarra to the wall of skulls.

The wall of skulls was just that: a long wall that was covered by a display of hundreds of Dire Wolf skulls. All of them had been found in La Brea Tar Pits and so all were the tell-tale coffee color. They were lined neatly in rows mounted in the wall-length, floor to ceiling, lighted glass, display case. It was truly a remarkable thing to see.

"Awesomeness!" said Shelly when she saw it. Dakota grinned at her use of his word. He knew it was Shelly's way of saying sorry for flattening his foot.

"Told you," he said.

And standing in front of the display was PaleoJoe. He was talking with a woman wearing a long white lab coat and as the kids joined him he introduced her.

"This is Dr. Beverly Hampshire," said PaleoJoe.

"Dr. Bev is a paleontologist on staff here at the Page Museum. Dr. Bev, this is my young assistant paleontologist, Shelly Brooks and her friend Sarra Fenniche. You already met Dakota Jackson, Private Investigator."

"Private Annoyance," said Shelly under her breath. Dakota elbowed her in the side.

"It's nice to meet you both," said Dr. Bev shaking hands with Sarra and then Shelly.

Shelly, as always, was very impressed to meet another paleontologist and she liked Dr. Bev right away. Beverly Hampshire was short and Shelly could look her right in the eye. Dr. Bev wore glasses with jeweled leashes attached to them so she could hang them around her neck, if she wanted to. Her eyes were wise and when she smiled at Shelly it was with warmth and interest.

"I've heard a lot about you, Shelly Brooks," said Dr. Bev. "PaleoJoe tells me that you are a very serious young scientist and have already discovered some wonderful and important things."

"Thank you," said Shelly feeling her face get a little warm under this praise. After all, she was currently in a bit of very deep trouble. It was nice of PaleoJoe not to bring that up just now.

"So I was wondering," said Dr. Bev, "if you and your friends would like to try a little digging right here at La Brea?"

"Would we?" Shelly's eyes went round with

excitement. "Just try to stop us!"

Dr. Bev laughed. "Follow me then," she said. "Digging for fossils at La Brea is really different from anything you have ever done before."

Shelly, Sarra, and Dakota excitedly followed Dr. Bev, but as she passed PaleoJoe, Shelly caught his stern eye and understood that, sooner or later, she would have to face the music of being in trouble. But for now, it would be later.

CHAPTER TWENTY-FOUR

PIT 91

Pit 91, adjacent to the Page Museum, was the only pit still being excavated at La Brea.

"Originally," Dr. Bev explained, "in the early 1900's, La Brea was surrounded by farmlands. Over the course of 40,000 years, layers of soil, debris and fossils built up and around the asphalt deposits making them many feet deep. As the fossil hunters excavated them they became cone shaped holes. That's how we got our nickname of Tar Pits."

Shelly, now wearing an old t-shirt and jeans and a bright orange hard hat, stood with her friends looking down into Pit 91. PaleoJoe was also wearing tar-stained clothes and a hard hat. Dakota and Sarra had decided to watch instead of dig. That was fine with Shelly. Digging required patience and she knew for sure Dakota had very little of that. Sarra wanted to look for her brother and Shelly understood that, too.

"We only dig in Pit 91 two months out of the summer," said Dr. Bev. "The asphalt is softer in the warmest months and easier to excavate. And anyway," she laughed, "we wouldn't have room to store all the fossils if we dug any more than that!"

The walls of Pit 91 were supported by steel beams and lined with tar stained boards. More planks and beams crisscrossed the floor of the pit. Shelly and PaleoJoe carefully climbed down a ladder into the Pit. Several people were already working. One of the workers finished scooping a shovel full of oozy black asphalt into a bucket and approached Shelly and PaleoJoe.

"Hi," he said and shook hands with PaleoJoe. "My name is Philip and I'll show you what to do."

Philip was a husky young man and had a deep California tan. Shelly could see a blond ponytail sticking out from under his orange hard hat. He looked like a wrestler thought Shelly, and he was covered with smears of tar.

"What were you doing with that bucket of goo?" asked Shelly.

Philip laughed and clapped a heavy hand on her shoulder, almost pushing her off the boards and into the tar. "I was glopping," he said.

"Glopping? What's that?" Shelly planted her feet a little farther apart to keep her balance in case Philip walloped her again.

"A thin layer of asphalt continually covers the

floor of the pit," said Philip. "We need to remove it so we can get at the fossils. So we use trowels to scrape it off the floor and then we glop it into buckets and haul it out. But, personally," Philip bent over and whispered behind his hand, "I think the stuff just oozes its way back in again."

"I see you have the site marked out in grids," said PaleoJoe. He was keenly interested in the process the workers were using and had been closely observing everything.

"That's right," said Philip. "You can see that bright yellow nylon cord we have stretched across the floor. That divides the Pit into a 3x3 grid."

"Very nice," said PaleoJoe rubbing his hands together. "How deep are you excavating?"

"Only to a depth of about 6 inches," said Philip. "We will wait until each grid is excavated to that depth before we dig deeper. It might take us awhile."

He trotted out along one of the planks motioning Shelly and PaleoJoe to follow him. "Come over here. Let me show you what I've been working on."

Philip knelt down on one of the boards where Shelly saw an array of tools spread out. There were a pair of small chisels, dental picks, soft brushes and a small jar of what looked like clear capsules the size of large aspirin tablets.

"What are those for?" she asked Philip.

"Even the very smallest fossils are important," said Philip. "They can tell us a lot about the environment.

We call them microfossils. When we find them we put them inside these gel capsules to protect them. Now. Just kneel down here. Careful, you don't fall in! And just look what I've found."

Philip steadied Shelly as she carefully knelt down beside him and pointed to one of the grids. And when Shelly saw what was in the grid Philip was working on she gasped in excitement.

"Look, PaleoJoe, a Sabertooth skull!"

Shelly and PaleoJoe knelt down beside Philip to get a closer look at the fossil he was uncovering.

"We have to be very careful of these fossils," he said. "They are fragile. We don't want to damage them by breaking them or scarring the surface."

"That's right," said PaleoJoe. "We can tell a lot by the surface of fossils and we don't want any damage from tools to interfere with that story."

"Here," Philip handed the brush to Shelly. "Go ahead and see if you can get any more of that uncovered."

Shelly took the brush from Philip and carefully began to work on the skull. She remembered what Karen Orchard had taught her on the *Stegosaurus* dig. She knew what to do.

"Very good," said Philip. "You're a natural."

Shelly smiled, but didn't look up. This was very delicate work. She had to concentrate.

Above the Pit, Dakota and Sarra watched Shelly and PaleoJoe for awhile. Dr. Bev left them to go and attend to other things. The day was hot and the smell of the asphalt made Dakota think of paving on the highways.

"I want to take a look around," said Sarra. "I want to see if I can find my brother."

"Okay," said Dakota. "I'll come too. I am an Ace at spotting spies. It's as though I have eyes in the back of my head!"

"Well keep them wide open then," laughed Sarra. "We don't want any surprises sneaking up on us."

But as they left the shelter of Pit 91 and headed back into the park toward the museum, one of the workers standing near the Pit exchanged his orange hard hat for a blue baseball cap and began to follow them.

CHAPTER TWENTY-FIVE

THE OLD BONE ROOM

Dakota went into Dexter North mode as he followed Sarra back to the museum. Walking just behind Sarra he turned his head constantly, sussing the crowd around them. Then, with unexpected suddenness, he whirled around to see if he could catch anyone following them. He couldn't see that there was, but in walking backward, he crashed into Sarra and knocked her over.

"Oh, sorry!" Dakota apologized feeling his face get hot. He reached a hand down to help Sarra regain her feet.

"It's okay," said Sarra brushing off her jeans. "Are you always clumsy?"

"It wasn't clumsiness," said Dakota, a bit indignant that this girl couldn't tell when he was sussing. "I was sussing."

Sarra gave him a confused look.

"You know—sussing? Checking things out?"

Sarra shook her head and her dark curls jiggled. "Sorry. But, look!" Suddenly she pointed over Dakota's shoulder. "There's Dr. Bev. Maybe she knows about my brother."

Dr. Bev was opening a door at the side of the museum. Ignoring the sidewalk, Sarra and Dakota sprinted over the grass in an attempt to reach her before she disappeared.

"Dr. Bev!" Dakota shouted.

But apparently she did not hear and, by the time Dakota and Sarra reached the door, Dr. Bev had disappeared.

"Rats!" said Dakota. "Well, let's go around to the main entrance. Maybe we can have somebody page her."

"Wait," Sarra grabbed his arm. "Look, this door did not shut tight. It is still open."

"Very cool," said Dakota. "Let's go."

Stepping through the door they found themselves not in the busy interior of the museum, but in a long dim corridor of closed doors.

"Oh no," said Sarra. "She could have gone into any of those!"

"Well, maybe someone saw her," said Dakota. "Let's find out."

They tried the first couple of doors, but they were locked.

"If she went in there, we can't follow I guess," said Dakota. But when he tried the next door he found it unlocked. "Awesomeness!" he said.

The room they entered was a large storage area. It was well lit and there were several people hard at work. And by the looks of things, Dakota decided that the work they were doing was indeed hard.

The room was filled with long tables, which contained jumbled piles of bones. But these bones seemed old and dusty. Boxes and containers littered the floor, spilled out from under the tables, and were stacked along the walls.

"Can I help you?" A tall teen-aged girl approached carrying a box filled with bones. She had two small silver rings pierced through her eyebrow. Dakota wondered if it helped her in the One Eyebrow Lift he so badly wanted to master. Maybe he would have to get his own eyebrow pierced.

"Hi," said Dakota. "We were looking for Dr. Bev and thought that she came in here."

The girl frowned and shook her head. "I haven't seen her."

"What is this place?" asked Sarra.

"This is the Old Bone Room," said the girl. "We are sorting through boxes of bones that have been stored here since the early 1900's."

"Why?" asked Dakota.

The girl laughed. "I suppose it does seem a little silly really, but actually we sometimes find cool stuff.

Come over here and I'll show you. My name is Fran by the way."

"I'm Dakota and this is Sarra. Do you work here?"

"I'm a volunteer," said Fran. "I don't live too far from here and I come over when I can. I'm kind of a geek, but I like bones."

"That's okay," said Dakota. "I have a friend who's geeky about bones too."

Fran smiled. She set her box down on a section of one of the tables. "It's fun to search through these old boxes. They are full of jumble mostly. See. I'm separating what I can." She pointed to several neat piles of bones on the table each labeled by a white card. There was a pile labeled "Fibias" and another called "Teeth" and one pile was labeled "I Don't Have A Clue." That was the biggest pile of all.

Fran carefully emptied her new box of bones onto the table. Some pieces of old paper fell out. "Sometimes we are lucky and these pieces of paper actually tell what's in the box." Fran squinted at the yellowing paper and shrugged. "Then again, maybe not. But you never know what you might find. A few years ago a volunteer found a skeleton of a *Homotherium,* which is a type of saber-toothed cat. Paleontologists did not know it had lived this far away from the mountains."

"All these fossils come from the tar pits?" asked Sarra.

"Yep," said Fran. "You can tell by the color."

Nearby a young man was using what Dakota recognized as a loupe to sort through a pile of sand.

"What's with the sand?" asked Dakota.

"Oh that isn't sand," said Fran. "That's a pile of microfossils. That's Brad. He's a volunteer, too. That pile he is sorting through contains tiny freshwater shells, minute bones, fragments of insect carapaces and plant material. The early paleontologists ignored tiny fossils or fossils that were broken or abnormal, but those kinds of fossils can really tell us a lot."

"Like what kinds of injuries an animal suffered from," said Dakota remembering his talk with PaleoJoe.

"That's right," said Fran.

"Are there many volunteers that work here?" asked Sarra.

"Yes," said Fran. "Quite a few, I guess."

"I think my brother works here. His name is Amine. Do you know him?" Fran thought a minute and then shook her head. "No. I'm sorry I don't know him. But I really only know the people who work in the Old Bone Room. There are a lot of other places he could work—Pit 91 or even in the Fishbowl."

"What's the Fishbowl?" asked Dakota.

"It's the lab up in the main museum," said Fran. "In fact, I bet that's where you could find Dr. Bev. Look, I'd take you there myself, but I should finish sorting this box."

"That's okay," said Dakota. "Just tell us how to

get there. We can find it."

So Fran gave them directions for finding the Fishbowl and ten minutes later Dakota and Sarra were completely and totally lost.

CHAPTER TWENTY-SIX

DEATH TRAP

"You don't know where we're going, do you?" asked Sarra.

"Yes, I do," Dakota lied. "The door we want is just ahead."

Somehow Fran's simple directions to finding the Fishbowl lab had gotten Sarra and Dakota hopelessly lost in the bowels of the Page Museum. Currently they found themselves walking down a long row of floor to ceiling cabinets. Intrigued, Dakota had opened a few drawers and discovered that they contained fossils. Some drawers were full of nothing but teeth. Another drawer was filled with tiny skulls. Another held hundreds of the tiny gel capsules that contained the delicate microfossils. As he hiked down the long row of cabinets Dakota thought it was incredible the amount of fossils that

must be stored in the vastness of the place.

"Well, I can't even see what's just ahead," said Sarra. "I just hope you are right."

Overhead dim fluorescent lights sputtered and the corridor stretched before them so far they could not see what was at the end of it.

"I'm right," said Dakota with fake confidence. "At least we know we aren't being followed."

But as he said it, he realized that even that wasn't true. Somebody *was* following them. They could hear the echo of the footsteps. Footsteps that were somewhere behind them. Footsteps that seemed to stop when they stopped, sped up when they sped up.

"Come on," said Dakota and began to run. Sarra was right on his heels.

Sarra and Dakota raced to the end of the corridor of cabinets. And finally, ahead of them they saw a door.

"I hope it's the way out," said Dakota.

But when they crashed into it they discovered that it was locked.

"Now what?" asked Sarra feeling panic rising.

"Wait! Listen," said Dakota and pulled Sarra down to crouch behind a low counter near the wall.

They tried to still their breathing. But even so, they could hear it plainly: the sound of footsteps running. Someone was chasing them.

"Come on!" Dakota grabbed Sarra's hand and they raced along the wall in the opposite direction from the pursuing footsteps.

Row after row of the tall cabinets loomed ahead, but Dakota thought he could see a distant red glow up high near the ceiling. *I hope it's an exit sign*, he thought.

It was. There was a pair of double doors and when Dakota and Sarra frantically crashed into them they burst open.

"Yes!" yelled Dakota and they burst out of the labyrinth of the museum into the bright outside. A short sidewalk led to another door in a building just ahead, most likely another branch of the museum. "That door will be locked," said Dakota. "Come on. We can't stay here."

He led the way, away from the building, across the museum lawn, and into an area of low scrub bushes and trees. There he and Sarra knelt down behind some screening bushes and spied out the way they had come.

As they watched they saw the doors burst open again and the figure of a man came running out. Dakota noticed the man wore a blue baseball cap pulled down so the brim cast his face in shadow. The man looked around as though trying to figure out where Dakota and Sarra had fled.

And then he started to walk directly toward

the scrub area where they were hidden.

"We can't stay here," whispered Dakota. "He'll find us. We have to run around to the front of the museum. We'll get back to where there are people. He won't be able to do anything then. Do you think you can run some more?"

Sarra nodded. "Who is he?" she asked.

"I don't know," said Dakota. "But clearly he's chasing us and I don't think I want to stay around here to find out why. Let's just back away slowly and then make a run for it."

"Okay," whispered Sarra. "You first."

And it was then that Dakota discovered an awful truth.

"Sarra!" he whispered, terror almost stopping his voice completely. "I can't move!"

"Neither can I!" Sarra eyes went wide with fear.

"We're stuck in tar," Dakota gasped. "It's a death trap!"

CHAPTER TWENTY-SEVEN

AN ENTRAPMENT EVENT

"Stay calm," whispered Dakota panic rushing through his veins like a high wind. "He doesn't know we're here. Keep quiet. Maybe he won't see us."

Maybe no one will see us, he thought. Maybe we'll stay here forever until we turn to fossils, too. But this wasn't happy thinking and so Dakota quickly tried to think of something else.

Beside him Sarra crouched and tried not to let her own panic cause her to hyperventilate. She closed her eyes. That helped.

They could hear the man enter the scrub. Twigs snapped under his feet and the bushes rustled as he moved through them. He was still heading right towards them.

And then he began to call out. "Sarra? Are you there? Is that you?"

"AMINE!!" Sarra's screech nailed through Dakota's ear because she was crouched right next to him when she realized who was after them.

She stood up and shouted and waved her arms. "Amine! We're over here! Help us!"

The man came crashing through the brush and, because he was moving so quickly, he almost ended up in the tar as well, but both Dakota and Sarra yelled at him so vigorously that, at the last instant, he was able to stop himself from treading into the seep.

"Sarra! I thought it was you, but I wasn't sure!" Amine grinned and waved his arms. "You have grown up so much!"

"Amine! I came to find you," said Sarra excitedly. "My friends helped me and I came all this way to find you!"

"And here we will stay unless someone knows how to get us out of here," said Dakota, pointing out what he felt to be the obviousness of their situation.

"Stay there," said Amine. "I can't get you out by myself. I'll go get help!"

And he dashed away.

"Right," said Dakota. "We'll just stay here, trapped in the tar, waiting and waiting and waiting..."

But Sarra was too excited to listen to him. "That was my brother, Amine," she said. "He's really here after all!"

"I noticed," said Dakota, looking glumly at his shoes covered with sticky tar.

"That was Amine following us all along and I didn't realize it!" said Sarra. "Don't worry, Dakota. Amine will get help."

"They'll probably have to chop our feet off to get us out of here," said Dakota, straining as hard as he could to lift his feet free of the seep. It was no good. They would have to wait for Amine to come back with help.

And about ten minutes later that is exactly what happened. Amine returned with Dr. Bev, Shelly, PaleoJoe, and about a dozen other people. Being careful to stay clear of the tar themselves, the rescuers used ropes and boards and eventually were able to pull Sarra and Dakota out of the tar. Dakota came out last and left one of his shoes stuck fast.

"Oh well," said Shelly giving him a quick hug. "Someday someone will find it and know that a boy with really stinky feet visited La Brea."

"Great," said Dakota without enthusiasm. "I always wanted to be famous."

Sarra had her brother Amine in a huge bear hug and it didn't look like she was going to release him anytime soon.

"This is my brother," she said to everyone. And Amine just hugged her back, a big grin on his face.

"Well, my goodness," said Dr. Bev. "I thought for a minute there we were going to have our very own entrapment event."

The rescuers from the museum who overheard this

remark laughed as they gathered up their equipment.

"What's an entrapment event?" asked Dakota, not really sure he wanted to know.

"I bet PaleoJoe can tell you," said Dr. Bev.

PaleoJoe stroked his beard and winked at Shelly. "These asphalt seeps are deadly," he said. "A lot of people think that the animals were trapped in deep pools of tar, but that isn't the way it worked. The asphalt seeps are really quite shallow, sometimes only inches deep. So let's pretend that Dakota was a large herbivore of the Pleistocene age."

"Right on," said Dakota grinning. "Just call me Sloth Boy."

"Dakota, the Giant Sloth, steps into a pool of water to drink and gets stuck in asphalt that is hidden by the water or maybe by dirt or leaves," said PaleoJoe.

"Just like the one we got stuck in," said Sarra.

"Right," said PaleoJoe. "And so then Dakota, the Giant Sloth, begins to yell and scream."

"Who wouldn't?" asked Dakota. "I bet anyone would."

"Exactly," said PaleoJoe. "Only instead of bringing Amine to the rescue, these yells attract other predators. First to descend are the meat-eating birds, like the eagles. They accidentally dip the tips of their wings into the tar and cannot fly off. They add their screams to the cacophony."

"That's a loud and annoying sound, in case you didn't know," said Shelly informatively.

“I knew,” said Dakota. “You’re looking at the expert of all things cacophonous.”

“Because they can’t get free from the tar, the animals die,” said PaleoJoe.

“Good-bye Sloth Boy,” said Shelly pretending to shed a tear.

“Then the predators move in,” continued PaleoJoe. “They in turn get stuck and when they die the scavengers try to get what they can, but they, too, are trapped.”

“And die,” said Shelly.

“You really enjoyed that didn’t you?” said Dakota. Shelly smirked at him.

“An Entrapment Event,” said Dr. Bev. “But they only happened about once every ten years or so. And happily this one turned out all right today. Now, Amine, I think we should all go into my office for a little chat. I know that there is some mystery here and I, for one, would like to know all about it.”

For a minute Amine looked a little concerned, but Sarra stepped up beside him. “Amine, these are my friends. I told them about the box of fossils you had.”

“You knew about that?” asked Amine in surprise.

Sarra nodded. “I am the one who took the big teeth out.”

And then Amine laughed. “Well, that’s one mystery solved for me,” he said. “Come on. I guess I’d better tell you the rest.”

CHAPTER TWENTY-EIGHT

ALL THE THINGS THAT CANNOT BE SEEN

Amine told his story to Sarra, Shelly, Dakota, PaleoJoe, and Dr. Bev when everyone got settled in Dr. Bev's office at the museum.

"Grandfather sent me on a simple mission," he said. "All I had to do was return the Smilodon skull to Miss Phoenix. It was hers, you see. He had made it for her. He still felt very badly about the disagreement they had long ago. Before he died he wanted her to know he was sorry.

"So I came to America and found Miss Phoenix. I gave her the skull, but when I opened my box I discovered the canine teeth were missing. I thought someone had stolen them. I worried about it because

I didn't want to get into trouble for smuggling fossils. Then I had to get a job to earn money to get back to Morocco. Miss Phoenix suggested I get a job here at the museum. When I did, I discovered the Smilodon skull in the case in the lobby."

"The closed-mouth skull with the missing tooth?" asked Dr. Bev.

Amine nodded. "When I saw that, I remembered something my Grandfather had said and I suddenly understood what had happened. You see, it was Grandfather who found the original skull."

"The unknown oil field worker," said Dr. Bev.

"That's him," nodded Amine. "And the thing Grandfather had said to me before I came here was that, after he had that replica of the closed-mouth skull made for Miss Phoenix, he may have gotten the real bones mixed up with the replica bones."

"We discovered that one of the canines that Sarra had was a fake," said PaleoJoe. "But the other one was real."

"I thought as much," said Amine. "What I figured out was that maybe the skull in the museum exhibit was a forgery and that I had the real skull."

Dr. Bev frowned. "I suppose that's a possibility. No one has ever really tested that skull for a fake."

"Your skull here in the museum is missing one of its teeth," said Amine. "And the skull I had, had both canines intact. That's why I thought it must be the real skull. I decided I needed to find a way to switch the skulls, because I knew that's what Grandfather would have wanted. And because I didn't want to be accused of fossil smuggling, I decided I wouldn't tell anyone about it, but would just find a way to do it.

"Only, as you can see, it's been awhile and I still haven't found a way."

"Well," said PaleoJoe. "I think the first thing we should do is to determine if the skull you have, Amine, is real or faked. Where is it?"

"Miss Phoenix has it," said Sarra. "I saw it on her shelf in the Wonder Room."

Amine nodded. "That's right."

"And I have the canines in my bag, which is also with Miss Phoenix," said Sarra.

"Good," said PaleoJoe. "We can take a look at the skull, see if it's real or fake and then see if Sarra's real tooth is a match."

So with this as the plan of action, Shelly called for Mr. Byrd and his taxi. Dr. Bev was unable to go with them, but she made them promise to call her as soon as they discovered anything.

When Mr. Byrd came, they all piled into his taxi. PaleoJoe and Dakota sat in the front seat. PaleoJoe and Mr. Byrd sang loud duets as Mr. Byrd drove through the late afternoon Los Angeles traffic and everybody else began to get headaches, especially Dakota who was sitting between them.

When they finally arrived at 2314 Orange Terrace, Shelly thought she might have to start screaming, but then all settled down as soon as Mr. Byrd and PaleoJoe stopped singing.

Miss Phoenix was delighted to see so many people on her front doorstep. She hugged Amine and scolded him for staying away so long and invited everyone inside. Shelly enjoyed the startled look on PaleoJoe's face when he met Cornelious Rathmorgan the Second. But it wasn't anything to the look on his face when Miss Phoenix showed them all into her Wonder Room.

Miss Phoenix stood to one side and allowed her visitors to browse her shelves of wonder. PaleoJoe went at once to a shelf of small fossils and Dakota became fascinated with a collection of spear points and arrowheads.

"So what do you think of my collection?" Miss Phoenix asked.

"I've never seen anything like it," said PaleoJoe. "It is the most wonderful collection I have ever seen."

"But it isn't all scientific," said Shelly.

"This bothers our little scientist quite a lot," said Miss Phoenix.

"I guess it doesn't have to be all scientific," said PaleoJoe.

"Why not?" asked Shelly. "What good is it if it isn't real?"

"You mean like the unicorn horn?" asked PaleoJoe.

"Yes, exactly like that," said Shelly.

"Well," said PaleoJoe, "here is what I think. I think that every scientist needs things of the imagination just as much as people who are not scientists do. And

I think that because without a strong imagination, it's hard to imagine possibilities."

Shelly thought about this for a minute. "And so you think that something like the unicorn horn is a thing of the imagination?"

"Yes, I do," said PaleoJoe. "Of course, now we know that the horn belonged to a narwhale which is a real creature and not a unicorn which is a made up creature. But wasn't the story wonderful just the same?"

"I suppose so," Shelly admitted and actually, when she came to think about it, she realized how much imagination, it took to think about what the world looked like when the dinosaurs were alive and even to imagine what the dinosaurs themselves looked like.

"So then we see, don't we," said Miss Phoenix nodding and smiling, "all the things that cannot be seen."

"And look," said Sarra going over to one of the shelves. "Here is the Smilodon skull."

Carefully she lifted it down and began to take it to her brother, but because she was looking at the skull and not where she was walking she did not see Gladiator where he was sleeping in the corner, until she stepped on him.

With a terrifying squawk Gladiator exploded into an angry flurry of feathers. Startled, Sarra dropped the saber-toothed skull and it when it hit the floor it shattered into pieces.

CHAPTER TWENTY-NINE

THE SECRET OF THE SABERTOOTH REVEALED

Gladiator ran squawking from the room, but the people he left behind were frozen in dismay. Slowly Sarra bent to pick up the broken pieces of skull. Shelly rushed to help her.

"I'm so sorry," Sarra stammered, her soft voice full of the tears brimming in her eyes.

"Oh goodness to me Sarah Jane," said Miss Phoenix flapping her hands as though brushing away annoying insects. "It's quite all right, child. Don't cry now. It was only an old bone."

But Dakota saw the look on PaleoJoe's face and he realized that the breaking of the skull was not a happy thing precisely because it was an old bone.

"It's okay, Sarra," Amine tried to comfort his sister. "It wasn't your fault."

"No, it most certainly wasn't," said Miss Phoenix. "It was the fault of that brainless rooster. Here I spend all day finding a couple of very nice hens for him and what does he do? He hangs out in here! I ask you. Is that the behavior of a sane rooster?"

"Hey," said Dakota. "What's that?"

"What's what?" asked Shelly.

"My keen detective's eye has spotted something there – just under the chair." Dakota pointed

"Your keen detective's eye has spotted another fragment of the broken skull, that's all," said Shelly down on her hands and knees investigating Dakota's find. "But wait a minute," she said as her fingers touched something else. "There is something here."

She reached her arm further under the chair and grasped something that lay there. Bringing it out into the open she saw she held a small velvet pouch. It was dark blue and tied tightly together with a silky cord.

"What is this?" she asked.

"I think that belongs to Miss Phoenix," said Amine, a slow smile spreading across his face. "In fact, I'm sure it does!"

"Me?" Miss Phoenix frowned. "I don't think that's mine."

"All the same, I think you should take a look," said Amine.

Miss Phoenix shrugged her shoulders. "Well, far be it from me to argue with the young," she said and carefully took the little velvet pouch from Shelly. The knot seemed to be tight but she wrenched at it with determined fingers and finally worked it loose. She opened the pouch. Holding out her hand, she gently shook the contents into her palm.

"Oh," breathed Shelly as the contents tumbled out. "Sarra, this is just like your nestled dolls! A treasure within a treasure!"

"Wow," said PaleoJoe. It wasn't a fossil, but he was still impressed.

"Awesomeness," said Dakota just because he liked the word.

"What is it?" asked Sarra.

In the palm of her hand Miss Phoenix held a small cameo brooch. It was a delicate sky blue and the face carved in a creamy white on the top of it was a younger version of Miss Phoenix herself. Even Dakota could see the similarity. A miniature book, no bigger than a matchbook, lay beside the pin.

"Here dear," Miss Phoenix handed the tiny book to Sarra. "My ancient eyes can't read anything that small. You read it."

"This book looks like it was handmade," Sarra said as she carefully opened it. And this is what she read:

In all the world the treasure
most desired and envied
is the love of a very true friend.

For my true friend, Twila
From Cadi

"Oh Cadi," said Miss Phoenix and she went to the window and stood looking out at the gathering twilight for what seemed a very long time. Everyone stayed quiet allowing her to think and remember.

"PaleoJoe," said Shelly softly so as not to disturb Miss Phoenix. "Let's test the broken skull. I don't think it could have been the real one, do you?"

"No, I don't," PaleoJoe shook his head. "Come on. Let's check it out."

Shelly, Dakota and PaleoJoe left Sarra, Amine and Miss Phoenix in the Wonder Room and went into the kitchen. Shelly scooped up a fragment of the skull as they left. In the kitchen Dakota chased Gladiator from under the table and shooed him out into the garden where he could see two very prim looking white hens resting on a bench near a rose bush. PaleoJoe produced some matches and a pin. He handed the equipment to Shelly.

"You know what to do," he said.

Quickly Shelly heated the pin and set the point against a fragment of the broken skull. The pin sank into it and the familiar smell of melting plastic tickled their noses.

"The secret of the Sabertooth revealed," said PaleoJoe. "Well done you two!"

"So the museum has the real skull after all," said Dakota, feeling relieved that a valuable fossil did not lie in ruins on the floor in Miss Phoenix's Wonder Room.

"And I bet we're going to find that Sarra's real tooth fits it like a glove, aren't we?" said Shelly.

"Great Sauropods! This is very exciting," said PaleoJoe rubbing his beard happily. "I'm going to call Dr. Bev right now and tell her the news!"

PaleoJoe hustled out of the kitchen. Dakota and Shelly sat looking at each other across the table.

"Well, the Dinosaur Detective Club can chalk up another case solved," said Dakota. "I wonder if Miss Phoenix has any cookies in her kitchen?"

"Dakota," said Shelly. And then she stopped. How could she say what she wanted to say? She wanted to tell him she was sorry about the way she had acted over the essay. And she wanted to tell him congratulations for winning. But Dakota was such a goof and what she had to say was serious.

And then she spied a kitchen towel on the counter. Suddenly she knew exactly how she could tell Dakota the things she wanted to say. Casually she stood up and, as though not even thinking about it, she picked up the towel. By the time she started twirling it up Dakota had realized her intention and was half way out the door to the garden.

Swick! The towel snapped just inches from Dakota's backside.

"Shelly!" he yelled. "I'm unarmed! That's not at all fair!"

"Oh it's fair all right," shouted Shelly winding up the towel again and charging out the door after him. "And you deserve it Dakota Jackson! You really deserve it!"

Miss Phoenix, watching the chase from the window of her Wonder Room suddenly smiled.

"Thank you, Cadi," she murmured. "Thank you, my friend."

And the peaceful evening at 2314 Orange Terrace was interrupted by the feathery squabble of disturbed chickens, the boisterous chase of Dakota Jackson by a shrieking, laughing Shelly Brooks and the sharp *thwick* and *snick* of a kitchen towel aimed with alarming accuracy.

"Ow!" yelled Dakota learning impressive new moves of evasion as he and Gladiator ran for their lives.

The End

About PaleoJoe

PaleoJoe is a real paleontologist whose recent adventures included digging in the famous Como Bluff for Allosaurus, Camptosaurus, and Apatosaurus. A graduate of Niagara University, just outside of the fossil rich Niagara Falls and Lewiston area of New York, Joseph has collected fossils since he was 10 years old. He has gone on digs around the United States and abroad, hunting for dinosaur fossils with some of the most famous and respected paleontologists in the world. He is a member of the Paleontological Research Institute and Society of Vertebrate Paleontology and is the winner of the prestigious Katherine Palmer Award for his work communicating dinosaur and fossil information with children and communities. He has given over 300 school presentations around the country.

He is also the author of *The Complete Guide to Michigan Fossils* and *Hidden Dinosaurs*.

About Wendy Caszatt-Allen

Wendy Caszatt-Allen is a teacher, poet, and playwright. She teaches 8th grade language arts in the Mid-Prairie Community School District in Iowa. A graduate of Interlochen in 1980, and of Michigan State in 1984, she went on to complete an MA at the University of Iowa. She is currently working on a Ph.D. in Language, Literacy, and Culture at the same institution. Recently her poetry has appeared in the Dunes Review. In addition, several of her plays for middle school players have been produced and performed on stage as well as appearing on local television. She has given presentations at the Iowa Council of Teachers of English and Language Arts and at the National Council of Teachers of English on reading and writing with adolescents.

She is releasing *Adventures of Pachelot: Last Voyage of the Griffon* and *The Beaver Wars* in 2007 with Mackinac Island Press.